Getting Even

Getting Even

ReShonda Tate Billingsley

Pocket Books
New York London Toronto Sydney

Pocket Books
A Division of Simon & Schuster, Inc.
1230 Avenue of the Americas
New York, NY 10020

First Pocket Books hardcover edition April 2008

POCKET and colophon are registered trademarks of Simon & Schuster, Inc.

For information about special discounts for bulk purchases, please contact Simon & Schuster Special Sales at 1-800-456-6798 or business@simonandschuster.com

Manufactured in the United States of America

10   9   8   7   6   5   4   3   2   1

Library of Congress Cataloging-in-Publication Data

Billingsley, ReShonda Tate.
  Getting even / ReShonda Tate Billingsley. —1st Pocket Books trade pbk. ed.
    p. cm.
  Summary: Camille and Alexis find their happiness and friendship tested when they discover they are dating the same boy, a realization that teaches them important lessons about vengeance and also strains relations in their Good Girlz church group that includes Jasmine and Angel.
  [1. Friendship—Fiction.   2. Dating (Social customs)—Fiction.
3. Forgiveness—Fiction.   4. Revenge—Fiction.   5. Christian life—Fiction.
6. African Americans—Fiction.]   I. Title.
PZ7.B4988Ge 2008
[Fic]—dc22   2007047421

ISBN-13: 978-1-4165-5873-6
ISBN-10:   1-4165-5873-X

A Note from the Author

When I first began the Good Girlz journey, I just wanted to tell interesting, page-turning, thought-provoking stories that young people would want to read and their parents wouldn't mind them reading. I never expected the reaction that I got. The thousands of e-mails, the endless amount of feedback, the requests for appearances. It all reminds me just how blessed I really am.

So this book is dedicated to you—those young people who sent me e-mails saying they'd never read a book outside of school and had now developed a love of reading, thanks to the Good Girlz. It's for the young lady who sent me an e-mail saying the books had stopped her from running away and taught her that her life was a "Blessing in Disguise." It's for the woman who came up to me at a book signing with tears in her eyes because she'd never seen her daughter excited about anything, let alone reading. It's for all the wonderful people—young and old—who have validated my literary career with their positive thoughts and words.

A Note from the Author

Thank you. Thank you. Thank you. Your kind words make everything I do worthwhile.

Because of your support, I will keep the books coming. Look for my next Good Girlz installment as Camille, Alexis, Jasmine, and Angel continue to bring you stories that will entertain, inspire, and keep you coming back for more.

Until then, drop me a line and let me know your thoughts, and of course, visit me on MySpace at www .myspace.com/goodgirlz1.

Thanks for the love.
Peace.

ReShonda

Getting Even

1

Jasmine

"I think I'm in love."

I looked at Camille and let out a loud groan. Camille was always in love. She was the most boy-crazy girl I'd ever met in my life. "So what else is new?"

"No, I'm serious this time," Camille said, a gigantic smile spreading across her face. "This is for real."

"Mmmm-hmmm," I said, shaking my head and turning up my lips. "It's for real, huh? Just like Keith, Walter, and everybody else your boy-crazy behind has been with."

"Fine, then don't believe me. Just don't ask to be in my wedding," she sang.

"Whatever, Camille," I said as I plopped down in a

chair. She and I were the first ones to arrive at the Good Girlz meeting, which was taking place in the church's conference room. We were gathered for our regular Thursday meeting. The Good Girlz was a group that was started more than a year and a half ago by Rachel Jackson Adams, the first lady of Zion Hill Missionary Baptist Church. Rachel started the group here in Houston as part of some church youth outreach program. She'd come up with the name "Good Girlz" because, as she said, she "wanted us all to strive for the good things in life." But trust, we were all far from being good girls.

There was Camille Harris, who came to the group after trying to hide her jailbird boyfriend from the cops. The problem was, old naïve Camille didn't know he had busted out of jail. She bought his story about getting out on "good behavior" and had him livin' all up in her grandmother's house. By the time the cops caught up with him, do you know what Camille's so-called man did? He jumped out a bathroom window and left her to take the fall!

Anyway, after a week in juvie, the judge let Camille off as long as she participated in the Good Girlz.

Then there was Angel Lopez. I think she's the only one who came here willingly. She was about to run away because she was knocked up by some dude she'd slept with one time! Luckily, we talked her out of it (well, she did run away, but we brought her back home) and now she's raising her little girl, Angelica, with the help of her mother.

Alexis Lansing is the uppity one in the group. I guess that's because her parents are loaded, with a capital L. Her dad owns some hotels and her mother is a straight shopa-holic. Alexis came to the group to fulfill some community service projects for school, but after getting caught up in a shoplifting scheme (that's another long story), she had to keep taking part.

And then there's me, Jasmine Jones. Trust me when I tell you, I didn't want to be here. But since I was always get-ting in trouble and fighting (I have a short temper, but I'm working on it), Miss Rachel, who used to babysit me when I was a little girl, made me come. She thought talking with the group would help me. I needed to learn to deal with people and control my anger.

Anyway, we were the original members of the group. We'd had some other people come and go, but Tameka Adams, Rachel's niece, was the only one who'd stuck around. Tameka was cool—sometimes. She had done some foul stuff last year, but we'd forgiven her for it. For-given, but not forgotten, which was why she wasn't as close to us as she would have liked to be.

"Will you listen to me?" Camille whined, snapping me out of my thoughts.

I huffed because she was getting on my nerves.

"Listen to you for what? Next week you'll just be in love with somebody different. Whoever this is will be gone to-morrow, so why waste your breath telling me about him?" I pulled out my economics textbook and started trying to get a jump on my homework before the meeting started.

I didn't mean to be in such a funk with Camille, but—as usual—my brothers had made me mad before I came to the meeting. Not only did they eat all the spaghetti, leaving me only a handful of dried-up noodles, but then we'd gotten to arguing and my grandmother had made me clean up the kitchen by myself. She was always making me clean up something.

I was the slave in my family of one sister and three brothers. My sister was the oldest, but since she was never at home, everything always fell on me. So I'll admit it—I spent a lot of time in a pretty foul mood.

"Jasmine, listen to me," Camille said, once again trying to get my attention.

I groaned, closed my textbook, and crossed my legs. "Fine! Tell me about *the one*."

She smiled. "*The one* happens to be called Vic."

"What, is he in the mob or something with that stupid *Sopranos*-sounding name?" I snickered.

"Would you stop playing!" She eagerly continued her story. "You know when we had to perform at halftime last week at the game against Yates?" I nodded. Camille was on the drill team and had to go to all the games to perform. "He came up to me afterward and said he loved the way I worked my baton."

I rolled my eyes. "Oh please, he couldn't come no stronger than that?"

She ignored my comment. "He said he couldn't take his eyes off me. Anyway, I gave him my number, he called, and the rest is history."

"Hard to make history in a week," I mumbled.

"Would you shut up and let me finish?"

I shrugged. "I'm just trying to figure out how you're in love in a week."

"Why you always hatin'?" She pouted. I guess she was mad because I wasn't all worked up over some dude who would be history next week.

"What are you girls arguing about today?" Rachel asked as she walked into the meeting room. She looked like her usual together self. Her reddish-brown hair dangled in spiral curls to her shoulders. And she was dressed in black slacks and a beautiful forest green blouse. Rachel was old—almost thirty—but she was still hip.

"Oh, the usual. Camille's boy craziness," I replied.

"I am not boy-crazy!"

"Whatever." I flicked her off.

"You need to be talking about your community service ideas," Rachel chastised as she took her seat at the table in the front of the room.

"Of course. We've already talked about that," I said. We'd been looking at ways to beef up some of our mentoring activities and I was actually looking forward to some of the things we had planned. "We have some great ideas. We're just waiting on everybody else to get here."

"Well, wait no more," Alexis said as she walked in.

"So glad you could join us," Rachel said, motioning for her to take a seat.

"I had to go pick up Angel." Alexis pointed at Angel, who had walked in right behind her. "And you know when

I got there, she wasn't ready. She was going all ga-ga over the baby."

"Well, what would you like me to do?" Angel said, playfully rolling her eyes. "My pumpkin started walking today." She beamed as she sat down for the meeting to begin.

I couldn't wait myself. Anything so I didn't have to hear more about Camille's love life.

2

Angel

I pulled up my jet-black hair and fanned the back of my neck. This hot August sun was kicking my butt. Sweat was trickling down my neck, and my thin T-shirt was sticking to my back. I looked over at Camille, who was starting to sweat herself.

"So where is he?" I asked for the tenth time in the last ten minutes.

"He's coming. Just chill," she replied.

I leaned back against the car door. "I wish I could chill," I snapped. "It's hot as all get-out."

We were standing outside Camille's old Honda Accord at the corner on Lockwood and Bennington. Her air conditioner was broken, so we had parked and were outside leaning against the car waiting on Vic, Camille's new boyfriend. She was excited about me meeting him after he got out of football practice at Kashmere High School, where he was a senior. But at this rate, I wasn't going to be in any type of mood to meet anybody.

"He was supposed to be here fifteen minutes ago," Camille said, looking at her watch. "He's probably just running late. I called his cell phone, but it keeps going to voice mail. And he's not answering my text messages."

"Well, I'm going to get a Gatorade before I pass out," I said. I made my way into the convenience store and had just stepped back outside, drink in hand, when I saw four girls approach Camille.

"Is that her?" one girl with long blond braids said, her neck wiggling. She was a good six feet tall, and stocky. She looked like she used to be a man in another life.

A smaller, much prettier chocolate-skinned girl crossed her arms and nodded while smacking on a wad of gum. "Yeah, that's her."

Camille looked at the girls. "Excuse me. Do I know you?"

"Naw, but you 'bout to," the blond-braid girl said with major attitude. "I'm Shoshanna and that"—she pointed to the pretty girl—"is Keysha. See, Keysha is my cousin and when somebody messes with my cousin, they messin' with me."

The girl was two inches from Camille's face at this point. She towered over Camille, but Camille didn't back down. "I'm sorry, but I don't know you or your cousin."

Keysha finally stepped forward. "Oh, but you know my man."

"Who is your man?"

"Vic. I heard your voice mail message, then saw that text with you telling him to meet you here. So I replied, erased it, and came instead. I wanted to see the tramp trying to steal my man."

Shoshanna took another step forward. The other two equally manly looking girls followed. "Are you messing with my cousin's man?" Shoshanna cocked her head.

I stood watching in awe, not sure of what to say or do. *Walk away, Camille. Just walk away.* I was hoping she was getting the mental messages I was sending her.

"First of all, Vic ain't said nothin' to me about no girlfriend," Camille replied, obviously not getting my thoughts. She had an attitude herself. "So if you got an issue, you need to take it up with him."

"I'm taking it up with you," Shoshanna said, her finger pointed in Camille's face.

"What, you can't fight your own battles?" Camille said, leaning over and looking at Keysha.

My eyes grew wide. Did Camille have a death wish? These girls looked like they didn't play. And there were four of them. Even if me and Camille could take them, we couldn't fight them by ourselves.

"You don't need to worry about what I can and can't fight," Keysha said, getting worked up.

"Whatever." Camille threw up her hand, flicking the

girls off as she turned to walk toward her car. "Come on, Angel. We'll just catch up with Vic another time."

Before I could respond, Shoshanna had grabbed Camille by her ponytail and flung her to the ground. She pounced on Camille and started punching. Keysha and the other two girls quickly joined in as well.

I screamed at the top of my lungs. It didn't do much good because they had Camille on the ground and the only people who ran out of the stores were two teenage boys who began egging the fight on. I took a deep breath and readied for my beat down as I jumped in and tried my best to help Camille.

I don't know how long we fought. Let me correct that—I don't know how long me and Camille got the mess beat out of us. It seemed like an eternity. But I wanted to jump for joy when I heard the store owner come out and start shouting, "Call the cops! Call the cops!"

Several people started pulling the girls off of us, which wasn't easy because they were swinging and kicking like crazy.

"That's just a small dose of what's gonna happen to you if you don't stay away from Vic!" Keysha yelled as she jerked free from the person holding her and raced toward her car. The other girls quickly followed her.

Someone, I didn't know who, helped me and Camille up. I could taste the blood in my mouth and my whole body ached. As bad as I felt, Camille looked worse. Her hair was all over her head. Her blouse was torn. And there was a big, black bruise forming under her right eye.

"Are you all right?" some lady asked her.

I wanted to scream, "Does she look all right?" But I knew if I opened my mouth, tears would come rushing out.

"Call an ambulance," someone else said.

"No, I'm . . . I'm fine," Camille said, rubbing her bruised face. She was wincing from the pain.

"Miss, don't you think you should stay and file a police report?" the store owner asked.

"No, we just need to go," she replied, tears forming in her eyes.

"Camille, I really think we should wait on the police," I reasoned as I wiped blood from my mouth.

Camille just grabbed my hand and said, "No, let's go."

She all but dragged me toward her car. I didn't ask any questions or protest any more as I jumped in the front seat.

We were on the freeway and were finally calming down when Camille handed me her cell phone.

"Call Alexis and Jasmine and let them know what just happened," she ordered.

I did what she said. As expected, Jasmine was fired up. Jasmine is a reformed fighter. She wasn't really a bully, although with her size she could've been. Still, she didn't hesitate to fight. Over the past year, though, she'd kinda grown out of that. But still, she was roaring mad and definitely ready to throw down when I told her.

"Does Alexis know yet?" Jasmine asked.

"No," I replied. After listening to Jasmine rant and rave, I wasn't even in the mood to call Alexis. "My head hurts and I don't feel like telling the story again. You call her and tell her."

"Look," Jasmine said. "Tameka was supposed to come over so we could work on our science project, but I'll call her and cancel. I'm gonna have my brother drop me off at Alexis's house. Y'all just come meet me there. We need to talk about this."

She hung up before I could respond.

I told Camille what Jasmine wanted. She didn't protest either. She let out a long sigh, then turned the car around and headed back down the freeway toward Alexis's house. She probably was thinking the same thing I was: Our moms were going to blow a gasket when they saw us.

So the way I saw it, we might as well go to Alexis's because right about now, any place would be better than going home.

3

Jasmine

"Dang, girl, you look like you were hit by a Metro bus," Tameka said as Camille took off her sunglasses. She leaned in and examined Camille's face. "Did you at least get a lick in?"

Camille pushed Tameka away but didn't respond.

She'd had on dark sunglasses when she walked into tonight's Good Girlz meeting, but I made her take them off. It's not like Miss Rachel was gonna let her sit up in here with sunglasses on anyway. It had been only a day, but her eye was still bruised and dang near swollen shut. Looking at Camille's face, I found myself getting mad all over again. We had talked about the fight for hours but still hadn't agreed on what to do about it.

"So, what's up? We gon' try and find the girls that jumped you?" I said as Camille slid in the seat next to me. I'd seen Camille in enough bad situations to know she wasn't one to back down from a fight. But she wasn't the type to go looking for one either. Me, on the other hand, I grew up fighting—with my brothers, with people in my neighborhood, and with classmates who felt my size (I was almost six feet tall by the time I was fourteen) gave them cause to pick on me. Shoot, I'd even been kicked out of my last school for fighting. And although these days I didn't go looking for fights, I dang sure wasn't about to let somebody punk one of my best friends and get away with it.

"I know you're not just gon' let this slide," I continued.

Alexis, who was sitting behind us, leaned up and whispered, "Can I ask you guys what we're supposed to do when we find them?" Fear was all over Alexis's face. Angel, who was banged up, but nowhere near as bad as Camille, looked like even the thought of seeing Keysha and her crew again terrified her.

"Look," I said, throwing my hands up in frustration, "even if they were to kick our butts—which they won't—at least it would let them know we ain't scared of them. Now, I don't want to fight nobody, but we can *not* let them get away with this."

"And you think retaliation is the answer?"

We all turned toward Rachel, who had quietly slipped into the room and had obviously been standing back listening to our conversation.

"Miss Rachel," Alexis began.

She folded her arms across her chest. "Don't 'Miss Rachel' me. Start explaining. What is this talk about trying to get somebody back? Does this have anything to do with your fight, Camille?"

"H-how did you know about the fight?" Camille stammered. We all looked at Tameka, who was standing right behind Rachel. I had told her what happened when I called to cancel our science project meeting. I never in a million years thought she'd tell Miss Rachel, though. Every time we tried to give Tameka a chance, she turned out to be nothing but a traitor.

Tameka shrugged. "What was I supposed to do? She was standing right there when Jasmine called. I tried not to tell her, but you know she can tell when I'm lying. So I just told her the truth." She looked like she desperately wanted us to believe that she hadn't been a snitch.

I knew Tameka had a point, but it was just hard for us to trust her. When we were all trying out for a job to be host of a talk show for teens last year, she'd stolen my term paper so I wouldn't get a passing grade and would have to drop out of the competition. She had later apologized like crazy, but for me, once you stab me in the back, it's hard for me to trust you. And since I didn't really care for Tameka, neither did Alexis, Camille, or Angel, although we all still tolerated her.

"And I can't believe you're even suggesting that Tameka should have lied to me," Rachel said, snapping me back to our conversation. "Besides, what did you think I was going to say when I saw you two?" Rachel pointed at Angel and Camille. "Now explain to me what happened."

"Camille got jumped," Alexis quietly replied.

"Camille got beat down," I corrected, rolling my eyes. "And Angel caught some of it, too, when she tried to help."

"Oh, my goodness," Rachel said, walking over to examine Camille's eye. She moaned. "Who did this?"

Camille looked like she was about to cry, so I stepped up. "Some girl who claims Camille's new boyfriend is her man."

"Did you call the police?" Rachel asked as she turned her attention to Angel.

"No, I didn't. They kind of jumped us and took off," Camille replied. "I couldn't call the cops. I wasn't supposed to be there in the first place. My mom is going to so trip as it is. I was able to get out of the house without her seeing me by staying in the bathroom until she left for work. I didn't go to school today, but I have a test tomorrow so I have to go. And, I'm not going to be able to avoid her tonight because she's off."

"She needs to know what's going on. And then you are skipping school on top of everything else?" Rachel added before letting out a long sigh. "Well, are you okay? Did you go to a doctor?"

"No, I'm fine," Camille said, even though she didn't look it.

"What about you?" Rachel asked, motioning toward Angel. Angel rubbed her cheek, which was still bruised.

"I'm cool. My mom went ballistic, but other than that, I'm okay."

"Well, I know you all aren't talking about revenge," Rachel said, her hands on her hips. I didn't know why she was trippin'. From the stories I'd heard, when she was our age she was buck wild and never would've let somebody jump her and get away with it.

"Miss Rachel, I know what you're going to say," I said. "But we need to let those girls know who they're messing with. We can't just let it go because they'll think they can punk us anytime."

Rachel crossed her arms. I could tell she was getting angry by the way her eyebrows were furrowing. "And what, Jasmine, do you suggest you guys do?"

"Payback," I said matter-of-factly, as I leaned back in my chair.

"So what, you're the Crips now?"

I rolled my eyes at her sarcasm. "No, we're not a gang, but . . ." I let my words trail off. I could see there would be no reasoning with Miss Rachel, so why even bother?

"Look, girls," Rachel said, massaging her temples like we were giving her a headache. "I know what happened to Camille, and Angel is messed up, but retaliation isn't the answer. Especially if these girls are as violent as they seem. Do you honestly think that if you go and attack them, they'll let it rest at that? It won't end until someone is seriously hurt, or worse—dead. People don't fight the same as they did back in the day. Now fistfights end with guns.

And besides, what have we talked about in terms of revenge? What have I told you about how that's something we should leave up to God?"

"Okay, Miss Rachel, I know all that stuff we talked about, but let's be real here," I said. "We can not let them walk away like nothing happened."

"I kinda agree with Jasmine, Miss Rachel," Camille added. "I mean, I didn't do anything to that girl and I'm not going to let her think I'm soft."

Rachel exhaled in frustration. "Camille, who cares what she thinks? You know you're not soft. You have to learn to turn the other cheek."

"What if that one is bruised, too?" I mumbled.

"Have you all not learned anything?" Rachel replied. She took a deep breath. "You know, this is right on time because I was going to talk to you ladies today about forgiveness."

I let out a groan. Don't get me wrong, I love being a part of the Good Girlz. (I can't believe I'm even saying that, seeing as how I never wanted to join the group in the first place.) But sometimes the lectures Rachel gives us can get pretty boring. Honestly, I knew they had some meaning behind them and they did usually help out. I guess today I just wasn't in the mood to hear it.

"Let's put aside thoughts of the fight and focus on our lesson for today. What are some of the things you think you could never forgive somebody for?" Rachel said, taking a seat in the chair in the front of the room.

I was the first one to raise my hand. "Lying," I said,

rolling my eyes as I recalled how my mom had lied to me about my father. I had grown up thinking he was dead when it turned out he lived about forty-five minutes away from me. Then, when I went to live with him, I found out the truth behind all kinds of secrets and lies—mainly, that he knew about me but his wife didn't want him to have anything to do with me. So because of all the people who had lied to me in my life, I couldn't stand liars. "Oh, yeah," I added. "And stealing my money. I wouldn't be able to forgive that either." Shoot, I put the "po" in poor and let somebody try to take what little money I *did* have. It would be on.

Camille raised her hand after me and blurted out, "Stealing my man."

Rachel chuckled as she shook her head. "Your money and your man. Can we get a little deeper than that? Anything else you think is unforgivable?"

The room was silent. "Okay, let's deal with stealing, be it money, boys, or something else. None of you have ever taken anything that wasn't yours?"

We definitely didn't respond to that. We'd all gotten into a whole bunch of trouble last year behind stealing stuff.

"None of you have ever lied?" Rachel continued like she didn't really expect us to answer. We were quiet on that one, too. Tameka and Camille had gotten downright dirty and told a bunch of lies to get that stupid *Teen Talks* host job.

"Ummm, just like I thought." Rachel sucked her teeth. "Imagine if God had said those are unforgivable sins."

"No disrespect, Miss Rachel," I said, raising my hand, "but we ain't God."

"I'm not saying you are, but—"

"Here we go with the religious lecture." I moaned.

"You obviously need a religious lecture," Rachel snapped. "Because you 'bout to pay a personal visit to Jesus if you get smart with me again."

Rachel used to babysit me when I was a little girl, plus she was close to my family and wouldn't hesitate to put me in my place, so I mumbled an apology.

She shot me another disapproving look before continuing to ramble on about how we needed to turn the other cheek. Personally, my mind was churning full speed ahead—figuring out a way to make this Keysha girl pay.

4

Angel

I put the pillow over my head and buried my face in my mattress. My headache from the fight had finally gone away, but my daughter was about to give me another one. Angelica was hollering at the top of her lungs. My mom was nowhere to be found, my sister wasn't answering her cell phone, and I had no idea what to do.

I finally couldn't help it and just let out a loud scream. "Aaaaaaagggggghhhhhh!"

This motherhood thing ain't no joke.

I love my daughter to death, but being a teenage mom is hard. When I first found out I was pregnant, I briefly considered giving her up for adoption. My mom was the one really pushing for an adoption. She even went as far as trying to find a good home for my daughter. We went back and forth with that until I finally agreed with her. But when it came down to it, I just couldn't give my baby away. I know I messed up. I got pregnant my first time, losing my virginity to a no-good dog named Marcus who not only didn't even want to claim his baby, but tried to make me out to be some kind of tramp. To this day, he's only seen Angelica three times. And that was because his mama made him. But I'm cool with it now. He ain't gotta love my baby. I got enough love for her all by myself.

Right about now, though, I needed a break because I was about to straight lose it.

My mom does help me out a whole lot when it comes to raising Angelica, but believe me, she lets me know this is my responsibility. I reminded myself of that as I got up and walked over to the crib, picked Angelica up, and tried to comfort her. I checked her diaper, tried to feed her again, felt her head to see if she had a fever; nothing was working.

Finally, about twenty minutes later, I think she just tired herself out and fell off to sleep. Quietness finally filled our small, wood-frame house.

A relieved smile was forming on my lips when the telephone rang. I dove across my bed like a madwoman and grabbed the phone before it woke Angelica back up.

"Hello," I said hastily.

"Hello to you, too. Dang. Why you soundin' like that?" It was Alexis.

"I'm sorry. Angelica is driving me crazy. She just fell asleep and I didn't want the phone to wake her back up."

"Oh, I'm sorry. I was just calling to see what you were doing."

"What am I always doing?"

"Playing mommy."

"Girl, I ain't playing."

Alexis let out a chuckle. "I guess you're right about that." She sighed before adding, "So, what's up for tonight?"

I frowned. "What's always up? Diapers and bottles."

"Can't you get your sister or somebody to babysit? You know the Gents from Booker T. Washington are having their step show and party tonight. It's at my dad's hotel. I wanna go."

I envisioned Alexis, not a care in the world, draped across her bed, twirling the phone cord around her fingers, bored out of her mind. Of course she wanted to go to a party. She had no responsibilities and an unlimited supply of money. My life was a totally different story. "My mom is at work and I have no idea where my sister is." After the day I'd had, I could use a party, but truthfully, I didn't have the energy to get dressed, even if I did have a babysitter.

"I need to find me some new friends," Alexis whined. "Camille's eye is still black-and-blue and she said she's not going anywhere in public. Jasmine is babysitting her little brothers—again. And now you can't go. You guys are gonna make me call Tameka."

"Yeah, right, like that would actually happen." Even though Tameka was somewhat cool, she could be annoying and she just wasn't the type of person you hung out with on your own. Tameka was only bearable when another member of the Good Girlz was there.

"Well, look here. I have an idea," Alexis said. "Why don't we ask Sonja to babysit?"

"Your maid?"

"Yeah. I really, really want to go to this party. Sonja loves kids. I'm sure she wouldn't mind watching Angelica for a couple of hours."

"I don't know. It just doesn't seem right."

"Oh, come on, Angel. You never do anything. I'll pick you up. We can come back and bring Angelica here. Sonja used to be a nanny. She'll be fine."

I thought about it. A party did sound like fun. Especially since I couldn't remember the last time I'd been to one.

"Please," Alexis begged.

"A'ight, fine. My mom is going to be so mad," I added.

"I think you should just leave her a note and tell her you and the baby are spending the night with me. She never has to know Sonja was babysitting. It's not like Angelica could tell her."

I thought about it. She had a point there. "See you in twenty minutes," I said before placing the phone back on the hook.

Exactly twenty minutes later Alexis was pulling up in front of our house. She honked twice. I scribbled a quick note to my mom, then lifted Angelica out of her crib, trying my best to make sure I didn't wake her.

I got her nestled in her car seat, then situated myself in the back of Alexis's BMW.

"Dang, girl, you look cute," Alexis said as she surveyed my boot-cut jeans, black vest, and white long-sleeved shirt. "A little conservative for my taste, but still cute."

I laughed. "Everybody can't dress like Beyoncé."

Alexis flung back her honey-brown hair. "I guess you're right."

I looked at her outfit. As usual, she was wearing the latest Baby Phat gear. She always had the tightest stuff, most of it before it even made its way down to Houston, because her mom was always flying to New York for shopping sprees.

"I really need a party," I said, leaning back in the seat. I didn't get out much. Shoot, I probably shouldn't be getting out tonight but Angelica had totally worn me out today. She'd been cranky since I'd picked her up from the sitter's. Plus, that chemistry test had kicked my butt, so I could really use a night of fun.

"So did you check with Sonja?" I asked as we made our way back to her River Oaks neighborhood, in the rich part of town.

"Of course; I told you she'd do it. She was happy about it," Alexis replied.

"Are you sure?"

"Yes. Now chill," Alexis said as she turned up the new Chris Brown song on 97.9, The Box.

It didn't take long for us to get to Alexis's house and

after getting Angelica settled with Sonja, we were on our way to the party. Alexis popped in an Akon CD and we got hyped before we even got out of her neighborhood.

It took us about fifteen minutes to get to the party. Of course, Alexis, being the showboat that she is, had to valet park.

"You are too funny. Most ordinary teens would've just parked across the street," I told her.

"As you know, I'm no ordinary teen," she said as she handed the attendant her keys. "Besides, why would I do that when my dad owns the place?"

I shrugged. She was right.

Inside the party, the music was thumping and the place was packed. We had barely made it in the door when some guy grabbed my hand.

"Hey, li'l mamacita. You sho' are looking fine today," he said.

I looked at him, saw he looked like a bulldog in the face, and snatched my hand away. *"No hablo inglés,"* I muttered as I walked off.

Alexis grabbed my arm. "Girl, you are so stupid." She giggled as she surveyed the room. "Camille and Jasmine are gonna be sick they missed this," she added, bouncing to the sound of the music.

"You know, it doesn't make any sense for you to be dancing over here in the corner by yourself."

We both turned toward the husky voice that sounded like it needed to be announcing a car commercial or something. It was coming from one of the prettiest guys I'd ever seen. He was tall, built, and had a rugged, sexy look. He reminded me of the singer Omarion, braids and all. He was staring at Alexis as he slowly licked his lips.

"Maybe I like dancing by myself," Alexis coyly responded.

"Maybe I want you to dance with me," the guy said back.

"Maybe I need to know your name."

"Maybe I need to know yours."

"Oh, gimme a break," I interjected. "Would you two go dance already?"

They both laughed as he took her hand and led her onto the dance floor. They must have stayed out there through five songs. When Alexis came back over to where I was standing, her hair was plastered to the side of her face and the front of her shirt was wet.

"Ewww," I said. "The sweat. So not cute."

"Dang," Alexis said, looking down. "I didn't realize I was sweating like this. I cannot believe this. Yuck."

"Yuck is right. I'm surprised he stayed out there with you looking like that," I joked.

"Not only did he stay out there, but he slipped this in my pocket," Alexis said as she reached down into her jeans. She pulled out a small piece of paper and waved it around.

"What's that?"

"That would be Anthony's phone number."

"So that's his name?"

"Yep, he's from New Orleans but he lives here now. Is he fine or what?"

I leaned over and looked at him as he stood around talking to some friends. Besides his beautiful skin, he had a killer smile. "Definitely fine. I'll give you that," I replied.

"So you didn't see any cute guys?" Alexis asked, still stealing glances at Anthony.

"Yeah, I saw plenty of cute guys. But I guess they didn't see me. I guess I don't look hoochie enough," I said as I noticed some girl in a bright red spandex dress.

Alexis stuffed the number back down in her pocket. "Well, I was lucky tonight. I got a good feeling about this."

"Okay, now you're starting to sound like Camille." We both laughed as we enjoyed the rest of the party. By the end of the night, I was so thankful Alexis talked me into coming, because this night out was exactly what I needed.

5

Angel

I watched as Alexis stared at her reflection in the full-length mirror. With the exception of some loose skin here and there, her body looked near perfect.

She turned around and looked at her rear end. She could give JLo a run for her money.

"It's hard to believe that all of this was once covered in blubber," she said.

I just shook my head. Alexis was a cute size six, one hundred pounds lighter than she was two and a half years ago—so she told me. It had taken months of coaxing, but Alexis had finally been able to convince her father to let her get gastric bypass surgery. He had never heard of teenagers getting it, but after she brought him all the pages of research she'd found on the Internet, he finally gave in. Alexis had shared how part of her believed he let her have it to just get her off his back. But the other part knew the real deal. He did it because he was tired of people talking about his fat daughter with "the pretty face."

Alexis had griped that if she had a dime for every time somebody told her, "You sure are pretty for a big girl," she'd be rich. Actually, she *was* rich; or at least her parents were. Her dad owned a couple of hotels and was part owner of the Houston Rockets. But she said all the money in the world didn't make up for the loneliness she'd felt all her life. She had a sister, Sharon, who was autistic and lived in a special needs home. So it was basically just Alexis, her mom, and her dad in this big ol' house.

Sure, after she lost the weight and transferred to another private school, she had more than her share of friends. But they weren't true friends. She'd told me she didn't know what that was until she joined the Good Girlz.

Just as she turned back to the mirror, there was a knock at the door. "What's up, chicken butt?" Camille said as she pushed her way in the room. Jasmine and Tameka were right behind her.

Jasmine looked at Camille and rolled her eyes. "You are so corny."

Camille gave her the hand, then came in and plopped down on the bed. "Let's get this party started."

Jasmine stood staring at Alexis. "Ummm . . ."

"What?" Alexis said.

Jasmine pointed to her body. "You think you want to put on some clothes?"

Alexis looked down. She was still in her bra and panties, and the look on her face told us she hadn't even realized it.

She laughed as she grabbed her sundress and slid it over her head. "Y'all are early."

"My mom started cleaning up. I had to get out of there before she made me help," Camille said.

"And you know Camille is my ride," added Jasmine.

"And mine," Tameka said.

"It's all good," Alexis said. "You guys hungry?"

"As all get-out," Jasmine replied while picking up some M&Ms Alexis had on the dresser and popping them into her mouth.

"Let's go downstairs and order a pizza." Alexis led the way into the kitchen. She pulled the phone book out, ordered two large pizzas, then popped in her copy of *Dreamgirls*. Tonight was part of the social time Rachel encouraged us to have each month.

Jasmine picked up the remote.

"Why we gotta watch this singin' movie? I mean, Jennifer Hudson is all that, but don't we have a scary movie or something?"

"You're outvoted," Camille said, snatching the remote away and pressing Play.

Both Tameka and I giggled as we sat down on the floor in front of the big seventy-two-inch television.

While the opening credits were rolling, Camille stretched out on the other sofa with a big grin across her face.

"What is your problem?" Jasmine asked her. "And why are you grinnin' all crazy?"

"Just thinking about my boo," she responded.

Jasmine rolled her eyes as she shook her head. "Y'all and these boys are 'bout to get on my nerves."

"Don't hate," she said.

Alexis sat down next to Camille. "I know what you mean, girl. I think about Anthony all day, every day. I think he's the one."

"Gimme a break," Jasmine said.

"Oh, she's just mad because she hasn't had a man since Donovan dumped her," Camille joked.

"Donovan did not dump me."

I hoped they would change the conversation because I knew Jasmine was sensitive about that whole situation. She was crazy about Donovan. They'd gone together for six months. He'd graduated and gone to the University of Texas at Austin on a basketball scholarship. They didn't last two weeks into the first semester. Jasmine never let on but I knew she was sick about it.

"When are we going to get to meet these guys?" I jumped in, trying to change the subject before Jasmine got mad and ruined the whole night. "I know I met Anthony, but I haven't had a chance to really feel him out, make sure he's legit," I joked.

"Let's all go out to eat this weekend," Alexis suggested. "I mean, I've been with Anthony for three weeks. It's time we all hung out."

"That sounds like a great idea," Camille replied. "Everybody can bring their dates."

"Aww, man. I have to go out of town this weekend," Tameka said.

No one responded. Probably because no one really cared whether Tameka came or not. But we were trying to include her more, so it's not like we'd ever tell her that.

"Oh, maybe you can go next time, then," Alexis said. "But you can all still go." She pointed to the rest of us.

Me and Jasmine looked at each other like, who were we supposed to bring? I hadn't had a boyfriend since Marcus, Angelica's father, and I don't think he even really counted since he didn't have two words to say to me after I slept with him. Now, all my time was spent raising Angelica—I didn't have time for boys. Neither Camille nor Alexis seemed to be fazed, though—they kept babbling about how they couldn't wait for the weekend.

"You're going to love Vic," Camille said.

"And you're going to love Anthony," Alexis replied.

"And I'm already hating this whole lovefest," Jasmine snapped. "So would y'all shut up so I can hear Jennifer Hudson tell me she's not goin'?"

Camille laughed as she threw a pillow at Jasmine. The

next thing I knew we were all caught up in a pillow fight. This was the life. A Saturday night, kicking it with my girls. I couldn't ask for anything better. It almost made up for the fact that I didn't have a Vic or an Anthony. Almost, but not quite.

6

Jasmine

"Pssst."

I sat up at my desk and cut my eyes at Camille. *I know she's not trying to get my attention in the middle of a test.* I ignored her and turned my attention back to my paper.

"Jasmine, what's the answer to number three?" she whispered.

I looked at her like she had lost her mind. Mrs. Reed's history class was the *last* place you'd ever think about cheating in. She'd have both of us expelled if she caught us.

"Jasmine, do you hear me talking to you?" Camille repeated. "Move your paper over so I can see it."

Even though Mrs. Reed had stepped out in the hallway and was talking to an upset parent, Camille must be on crack if she thought for a minute that I was about to help her cheat. Mrs. Reed had spies all throughout her room. It wasn't my fault Camille hadn't studied for this test.

"Oh, so it's like that?" Camille hissed. "You're not gon' tell me the answer?"

I sighed. "It's B. Now leave me alone." I just wanted her to shut up before we both got into trouble.

"And what's the answer to number six?"

I swear, it was getting more and more difficult for me to step away from my violent ways because right about then I wanted to knock Camille in her jaw. "Shut up and leave me alone," I said through gritted teeth. I glanced outside to make sure Mrs. Reed was still engaged in her conversation. She was, but seemed like she was about to wrap it up.

Camille was just about to lean in and whisper something else to me when thankfully Mrs. Reed walked back into the room. "You have five more minutes on the test," Mrs. Reed announced.

I answered the last five questions, then set my pencil down. I was actually happy that I knew the answers for a change because I definitely wasn't the greatest in school. I was a B and C student at best. Not that I didn't try, I just had all this stuff going on at home. Camille was the A student, but ever since she started hanging out with Vic, her mind had been all wrapped up in him.

"Miss Harris, can you take up the papers, please?" Mrs. Reed told Camille.

Camille groaned as she stood up and started collecting the tests. She reached over to take mine and snatched it out of my hand. I stuck my foot out and made her trip. The whole class, including me, busted out laughing.

After class, Camille gathered her books and headed straight to the door. I caught up with her just outside in the hallway.

"So you not speaking to me now?" I said.

Camille spun around and shot me an evil look. She looked tired, like she hadn't gotten a good night's sleep. And both the T-shirt and jeans she had on looked like they needed ironing.

"What is your problem?" she asked.

I folded my arms across my chest. No, she wasn't catching an attitude with me because I didn't want to chance getting expelled. "I should be asking you that. Why are you trippin'? I know you're not mad about me not giving you the answers. You know I normally don't have any problem helping you out but I can't be caught cheating, especially in Mrs. Reed's class. My mom would go ballistic if I got kicked out of school again." I already had to transfer from one school for fighting. My mom's not trying to hear nothing about me getting kicked out again.

Camille sighed. She knew I was right but she said, "You know you coulda given me those answers."

"You know you coulda studied." I turned and started walking down the hall toward my Spanish class.

Camille rolled her eyes as she followed me. "Fine. But I so flunked that test."

I stopped and turned to her. "Which I don't understand. History is your best subject. You know this stuff. What's goin' on? I mean, did you even open the book?"

She smiled. "Me and Vic were on the phone and the next thing I knew, it was eleven o'clock. My mom was trippin' about me going to bed. Then she asked me if I had studied. Of course I didn't tell her I hadn't. So she made me turn off the light and go to sleep. As soon as she left, I called Vic back and we fell asleep on the phone together. I thought I could study this morning, but I woke up in just enough time to get to school."

"All right. Vic seems cool and all, but don't let him have you flunking out of school," I warned. I'd met Vic twice now and Camille was right—he was cute, fun, and so into her. But still, she didn't need to be messing up at school behind him.

"Yeah, yeah, yeah," she replied. "Anyway, he's game for us all going out this weekend. How does Papacita's sound?"

I stopped just outside the door of my next class. "It would sound great—if I was going." I'd already told them I wasn't coming because Angel wouldn't be there and I was not about to be the only one sitting there without a date.

"Hey, I got that taken care of. Unlike you, I look out for my friends," Camille joked. "I got a date for you."

I twisted up my lips. "Girl, please. I'm not about to go on a blind date."

"Come on. Vic says Rodney is cool."

"Have you ever seen Rodney?"

"No, but—"

"Well, then, I ain't going."

"Please, pretty please," she begged. I was grateful when the tardy bell rang.

"Nope today, nope tomorrow, nope anytime you ask me. I gotta go."

I dashed into my class before she could say another word. But I knew Camille. She wouldn't stop bugging me until I gave in. So I prepared for my first blind date.

7

Angel

I watched as Alexis tried on her sixth outfit. "So what about this one?" she asked.

I sighed as I flipped through the latest issue of *Right On!* magazine. "It's cute just like the others," I said, not bothering to look up.

"You don't think it makes me look too fat?"

I finally glanced up at her. "No, Alexis. You are nowhere near fat, okay? And you have seven thousand outfits," I said, pointing to her walk-in closet that was the size of my whole bedroom. "Why are you acting like it's so hard to find something to wear?"

"Because I have to find the perfect outfit."

"Well, you already have the boy's nose wide open so

I don't know why you're trippin'." I'd gone with her to meet Anthony one day last week and he'd been all over her.

Alexis smiled as she wiggled her hips. "I guess you're right. I can't wait for Camille and Jasmine to meet him. They're going to love him."

"I'm sure. You all have fun."

"You know you can still go."

"I told you. I'm with Jasmine. I don't want to be the only one without a date."

"I told you Camille found Jasmine a date."

"Oh, yeah, well, I don't want anybody *finding* me a date. My prince is coming and until he does, I'll just spend time with my baby."

Alexis walked over to the edge of the bed. "Come on, Angel. You're too young to be a homebody. I know you have to be a mother and all, but that doesn't mean that you can't have fun."

"I have fun. But not with some buster y'all have to fix me up with."

"Whatever," Alexis said as she grabbed her hair, pulled it up on top of her head, and walked over to look at herself in the mirror. "Should I wear my hair up or down?" She cocked her head to the side.

I studied her for a minute. "Wear it down. Up makes you look too old."

She moved her hands and let her hair drop as she flung it out. "I guess you're right. And I think I'll go with the pink outfit," she said, picking up the first thing she'd actually tried on. "What time is it anyway?" she asked, holding the outfit up to herself in the mirror.

"Time for you to hurry up if you're going to drop me off and get over to Papacita's by seven." Camille had actually arranged this dinner and they were probably going to have a blast, but they'd just have to tell me all about it tomorrow.

Alexis was just about to say something when her phone rang. "Can you get that for me?"

I reached across the bed and picked up her pink princess phone, which matched every other pink thing in her room. "Alexis's residence," I said, once again feeling a tinge of jealousy that she was one of the few people I knew with her own private line.

"Yo, can I holla at Alexis?" the voice said.

"Yo, who's calling?" I replied.

He laughed. "The only dude that betta be calling."

"Oh, hi, Anthony. This is Angel."

"What's up?"

"Nothing much. Hold on." I handed the phone to Alexis. "It's your prince."

She smiled as she took the phone. "Hey, baby. I'm going to drop Angel off, then I'll be by there to get you."

I did know that while Anthony had a small truck, like most guys Alexis dated, he would much rather roll in her BMW.

I watched as Alexis paused, the cheesy grin leaving her face.

"What?" she said. "Your mom can't find anybody else?"

43

She paused again, a sad look crossing her face. "No, I understand. I hope your grandmother gets better. Okay. I'll talk to you later."

Alexis looked like she had tears forming in her eyes as she put the phone back on the hook.

"What's wrong?" I asked.

"Well, it looks like I'm dateless tonight, too."

"Why? What happened?"

"Anthony can't go. His grandmother is sick."

"He doesn't strike me as the type to care for a sick grandmother," I said. Something didn't sound right to me.

"He's sweet like that," Alexis said, hanging the pink outfit back up. "He said his mom had to work and his grandmother is really sick so he can't go. Let me call Camille and let her know."

"Camille's cell phone is broken, remember?" I said. "She dropped it in the sink."

"Oh, yeah," Alexis said, putting the phone back down. "I guess that means I can't text her either. Dang. Jasmine really needs to get a cell phone."

I laughed. "Yeah, right. Jasmine barely has a house phone."

Alexis laughed, too, as she slipped into her clothes, then grabbed her car keys.

"So what are you going to do tonight?" I asked.

"I'm not going to be a third wheel. I guess I'll just come back and study. I have a geography exam I need to be studying for anyway."

I gathered up my things. "Maybe after you drop me off

you can go by the restaurant. That way they're not sitting up there wondering where you are."

"Yeah, I guess I could do that," she replied with a heavy sigh. "Man, I really wanted them to meet Anthony."

"Well, we can do it another time. There will be other opportunities."

"Yeah, I guess." She smiled. "Come on, let me take you home."

We were headed to my house when Alexis pointed right off the freeway. "There's Papacita's. Let's just run in and let them know I'm not staying. I can at least meet Vic real quick."

"Sure," I responded.

We pulled in the parking lot and luckily found a spot right up front. We walked inside and the hostess immediately greeted us.

"Hi, welcome to Papacita's Restaurant. Will it be two today?" she said.

"No, we're just looking for some of our friends," Alexis said.

"Okay," the hostess replied. "Feel free to look around."

We walked around the restaurant for a few minutes, with no luck. "I guess they're not here yet," Alexis said, looking at her watch. "It's ten after seven. You know Camille is always late. I guess I'll just leave a message the old-fashioned way."

Alexis walked back over to the hostess stand. "May I have a piece of paper?"

The hostess smiled as she handed Alexis a blank sheet

of paper. Alexis scribbled a note, then handed it to the hostess. "My friend and her date are coming. Her name is Camille Harris. She's about my height, brown skin, and has spiral curls. They should be here any minute now. Can you make sure she gets this?"

The hostess nodded as she took the note.

Alexis and I made our way back to her car. I could tell Alexis was still bummed out. I guess I would be, too, if I'd found the perfect guy and all my friends had yet to meet him. But I was sure Camille and Jasmine would get their chance, because from the looks of things with Anthony and Alexis, he wasn't going anywhere anytime soon.

8

Jasmine

I watched as the butter-colored boy dipped his half-eaten chip in the cheese sauce, dropped sauce all over his shirt, then popped the chip in his mouth. The way he was chomping on that chip, he looked like a cow chewing its cud, as my grandmother would say.

To say I was disgusted would be an understatement.

"What you staring at me for?" he asked, cheese sauce stuck to his two front teeth.

I couldn't even reply. I just shook my head and once again turned to Camille and shot her an evil look. I knew I never should've let her hook me up with this buster.

He was so disgusting he'd actually been a little entertaining at first. And believe me, I needed to be entertained because Camille and Vic were acting like we weren't even here. They were all over each other.

I kicked Camille under the table to try and let her know she better direct some of her conversation my way because the freak show sitting next to me was getting boring.

"Ouch!" She jumped and looked my way. I guess my expression told her exactly what I was thinking because she smiled and said, "So, Rodney, where do you go to school?"

He frowned like she'd said something disgusting. "Awww, man, school is for punks."

No, he didn't. This wasn't even funny anymore. Camille owed me big-time for this. I knew I shouldn't have come. This was all Alexis and Camille's idea so their boyfriends could meet and Alexis hadn't even showed up. The hostess had given us some note that Alexis had left, which said Anthony couldn't make it so she was bailing out on us.

Camille had begged and whined until I finally agreed to go out with one of Vic's friends. She had played up the whole "Rodney is tall with gray eyes" speech. She just left out the part about him being a tall, gray-eyed, Shrek-looking, nasty pig.

"What do you mean school is for punks?" I'd tried not to say anything. But I had to see if he was serious.

"Just like I said," he replied, grabbing another handful of chips and stuffing them in his mouth. "What I need all that stuff for? I can read and write and count my dough. That's all that matters. You is brainwashed if you think you need school."

"Maybe if you went to school, you'd know it's 'you *are* brainwashed,' " I snapped, rolling my eyes.

Camille cut her eyes at me. I didn't care. Not only was he ugly and disgusting, but he was dumb, too. *I don't think so.*

"Awww, you got jokes." Rodney laughed.

I wanted to tell him I wasn't joking, but then I figured, why waste my breath?

"You know, the way I see it, you go to school so you can get paid," he continued. "Well, I'm already gettin' paid. I'm all about the paper, baby. So you ain't even gotta worry about that. I'm gon' gets mine."

Spoken like a true drug dealer. I twisted up my lips. "Just how do you plan to 'get yours'?"

"That's personal and classified info-mation." He flashed his teeth, displaying a grill that might have been cute on Ludacris, but had him looking like a broke-down, wannabe rapper.

"Come on, you guys," Vic finally spoke up. "Let's just chill out and order some dessert." He cracked a joke and I actually smiled for the first time that evening. I liked Vic. He had a good personality and he definitely looked good. Maybe he'd brought this jerk along so we could see how tight he really was. He and Camille made a cute couple.

As if to drive home how different they were, Rodney let out a loud belch.

I shook my head, trying to ignore him. "No dessert for me. I need to get going. Camille, are you about ready?" I knew she wasn't, but I didn't care.

"Look here, shawty," Shrek said. "Why don't you let me take you home?"

I wanted to tell him I'd rather be run over by an 18-wheeler, but I just flashed a fake smile. "That's okay. I'm straight."

The waiter came over and placed the check on the table. Rodney immediately picked up the bill; for a minute, I thought he was going to show some class.

Boy, was I wrong.

"I had the chicken enchilada and a Coke. So my part is eleven twenty-eight. Jasmine, it looks like your part is, ummm, what's nine ninety-nine and two forty-nine?" Rodney said, looking up at me.

I couldn't do anything but stare back, trying to see if he was serious. He was.

He just shrugged and pushed the bill toward me. He took out a ten and two ones and laid them on the table. "I got the tip," he said, motioning toward his money. "She can just keep the change."

Wow, a whole seventy cents, I thought. "So, you want me to pay for my own dinner?" I asked as he rubbed his stomach.

I shot Camille a look to let her know I was going to kill her. I wasted my time with this jerk and I still had to pay for my own dinner.

It was his turn to look at me crazy. "You want me to pay and you won't even hang out with me for a little while tonight? Yeah, right," Rodney said as if reading my mind.

I couldn't believe this fool. I snatched up my purse and

opened it. I was straight frontin'—I knew I only had about four dollars to my name, but I didn't want him to think I was going to beg him for anything.

Camille must've known I was about to lose it because she reached for the check. "Don't worry about it, Jas. I got it. I invited you here, so I'll take care of it."

Vic took the check. "Naw, y'all, I got it." He frowned at Rodney, who didn't seem the least bit fazed. "Boo, you know as long as I'm around, I got you. And your friends." He lightly kissed Camille on the lips.

I looked at Camille and smiled. *Okay, I might have to agree with her on this one. This time around, it looks like she might have definitely caught her a good one.*

I took one last look at Shrek, who was actually sitting at the table scratching under his armpit, and thought, *Why can't we all be so lucky as to find a guy like Vic?*

9

Jasmine

I flung open the bathroom drawer and frantically searched for my MAC Oh Baby Lipglass. I had looked everywhere. I didn't wear much makeup, but I had come to love my Oh Baby.

I was heading to the Houston high school All-American basketball game and Donovan, my ex-boyfriend, was supposed to be there. He'd called me yesterday and asked me to come, so I wanted to make sure I was looking cute. I slammed the bathroom drawer shut after not finding the lip gloss.

"Nikki!" I screamed, yelling for my older sister. I stomped down the hall to the small bedroom that she and I shared. As usual, she was in the mirror, rubbing gel on that baby hair she loved so much. My sister was what you would call ghetto fabulous. Today she had loud burgundy hair pieces mixed in with her own jet-black hair. She had on a tight miniskirt and a low-cut blouse. She looked a plumb hot mess.

I shook my head at the sight of the blue eye shadow that covered her bulging eyelids. Then my eyes made their way down to her lips. She had lined them with black eyeliner, then filled them in with a beautiful lip gloss. *My* gloss!

"Where's my lip gloss?" I snapped.

"I don't know what you're talking about," Nikki said as she smoothed some gel on the baby hair on the other side of her head.

"You have it on! So don't lie." I motioned toward her mouth.

"Oh, this? I don't know. I just found it laying around." She pointed to the lip gloss on the dresser. "What's the big deal? I just used a little bit of your funky lip gloss."

I picked up the case and pulled out the brush. It was almost dry. "A little bit? You used more than a little bit!" That stuff wasn't cheap. Alexis had bought it for me for my birthday and I'd tried my best to make it last.

"So I might've been using it for the last two weeks. Since when did you start wearing makeup anyway?" she asked nonchalantly as she sashayed out of the room.

I followed behind her, furious. "I told you a hundred times, stay out of my stuff!"

"Okay, don't y'all come in here with that noise," my mother said. She was stretched out across the sofa after coming home from her day job. My mother worked two jobs—as a housekeeper at the Westin Hotel during the day and as a security guard at night. "I have a headache and I don't feel like hearing it. I've already sent your little brothers over to the neighbor's house. Your grandmother is at church and I just want some peace and quiet."

"Tell Nikki to stay out of my stuff!" I yelled.

Nikki ignored me as she leaned over and kissed my mother on the forehead. "Enjoy your quiet evening, Mama. I'm going out with Tony."

"Aren't you going to say anything to her?" I asked my mother.

She closed her eyes and covered them with a wet towel she had in her hands. "I don't hear you. I'm going to a place where there are no kids," she said, stretching out and getting comfortable.

"Uggghhh!" I said, storming back to my bedroom. Sometimes I absolutely, positively couldn't stand my life. Sure, I'd learned my lesson after trying to go live with my father and his family earlier this year. That life was even worse than the one I already have, but that didn't mean my family didn't still get on my last nerve.

I was still fuming when my brother Jaquan stuck his head in my bedroom door. "Look, Waterhead, I'm about to roll out. You betta come on if you're goin' with me," he said.

I knew I should've just told Alexis to come get me instead of riding to the game with my brother and his stupid friends. I sighed, then dabbed as much of the dried-up lip gloss on my lips as I could, grabbed my purse, then followed Jaquan downstairs to his friend Pretty Ricky's car.

As usual, Pretty Ricky—who really wasn't all that pretty, but liked to think so—made some obnoxious comment, and as usual I ignored him. "So when you gon' fix me up with that fine chocolate friend of yours?"

"Camille?" I asked as I climbed into the front seat. My brother and his freak-of-the-week were in the backseat. "Like she would ever want you," I said.

Ricky just laughed. "She gon' be there tonight?"

"No, she's probably out with her boyfriend," I stressed.

"Well, tell her I asked about her."

Whatever, I thought as I glanced back at my brother, who was already slobbering all over the girl, who hadn't even bothered to speak. I was so glad Jaquan and Alexis hadn't worked out. They'd started dating a few months ago, without my knowledge. Without selling him out, I had tried to warn Alexis that my brother was no good, but she wouldn't listen. As expected, he dumped her after just a few weeks and moved on to another girl. For a minute, it had caused some major problems between us, but we worked it out. Thankfully, she was over him in no time.

"So, what's up?" Ricky said. "Ya boy gonna be there?"

"What boy?" I said, knowing he was talking about Donovan. I looked back and rolled my eyes at my brother, who must've been eavesdropping on my call. That was bad enough, but then he had to go spreading all of my business to his friends.

Ricky laughed again. "So it's like that?"

I ignored him as we pulled into the Butler Stadium field house, where the All-Star basketball game was being played. We had to park way on the other side of the parking lot, that's how crowded it was. We made our way inside, but I kept my distance from my brother and his creepy friends. As soon as I got inside, I started scanning the room looking for Donovan and Alexis, who was supposed to meet me at the game.

I spotted Donovan first. He was standing over in a corner surrounded by a group of girls who looked like they just wanted to jump his bones. I ducked into the girls' restroom, gave myself a once-over, then made my way back into the gym. I casually passed by Donovan, trying my best to act like I didn't see him, but praying that he saw me. I breathed a sigh of relief when I heard him say, "Jasmine?"

The girls around him looked like they didn't appreciate losing his attention. But it made me feel good to know that he didn't care. He just walked over and hugged me.

"Hey, you. What's up?" I said, hugging him back. It felt so good to be in his arms. Donovan and I met under embarrassing circumstances: My grandmother had sent me to the grocery store with her food stamp card and just as I was about to use it, Donovan walked up. I almost died. Needless to say, I just left the groceries there rather than let him see me using a food stamp card.

He had transferred to my school after Hurricane Katrina destroyed his home in New Orleans. He and I had started kicking it and everybody and their mama was trippin' because Donovan was all that and then some. He was taller than me, which didn't happen very often since I was almost six feet tall myself. He had gorgeous hazel eyes, a closely cropped cut, and a body that could put Tyrese to shame. Matter of fact, to me, he looked like a taller, lighter version of Tyrese. A lot of people couldn't understand what he wanted with a tomboy like me.

We started going together and were doing good until he went off to college in Austin, about three hours from Houston. I guess since he was a superstar basketball player, he decided he didn't want a girlfriend and dumped me. Although he claimed he just wanted to focus on school and basketball, I knew it was because he got up there with all those college girls. At first I was mad. In fact, I hadn't even talked to him the few times he tried to call me. But standing there looking at him now, I couldn't be mad at all.

"Dang, girl, you look good," he said.

I smiled, trying not to blush. He always did have a way of making me feel beautiful, something no other guy had been able to do.

"You're not looking half bad yourself," I replied, trying to be girly and get my flirt on, which was really hard for me. But my girls had been working with me so I'd gotten a little better.

"Who are you here with?" he asked.

"Oh, I rode up with my brother but I'm meeting Alexis. What about you?"

"I'm here with some of my friends," he said, pointing over to a group of guys sitting in the bleachers. "Check this out, one of them is dating Alexis."

"For real? Anthony?"

Donovan nodded.

"Oh yeah, that's Alexis's new boyfriend. It's a small world. How do you know him?"

"He's from New Orleans, too. He transferred here after Hurricane Katrina."

"Oh. Well, I haven't met him yet."

"Cool, you can meet him now. And you can sit with me until Alexis gets here," he said playfully.

I smiled, grateful for the opportunity to spend some time with Donovan. I followed him to the bleachers.

"What's up, fellas? Remember my girl Jasmine? The one I told you about? I want you to meet her." He looked at me. "They've been ridin' me because I told them I was looking forward to seeing you tonight."

I fought off the butterflies in my stomach as he took my hand. I couldn't believe he'd actually told his boys about me, that he still talked about me.

"This is Lil Dave, Terrence, and Tyrone," he said, pointing to his friends. Each guy spoke.

"Where did Anthony go?" Donovan asked.

"He's over there, hollerin' at some girl," Tyrone said.

Donovan immediately shot him a look to tell him to shut up. "Ummm, Jasmine is Alexis's friend. You know, Anthony's *girlfriend,* Alexis," Donovan said.

Tyrone immediately got a look across his face like he'd said too much. I fought back a laugh. I'd have to let Alexis know her man was off flirting, even though it was probably nothing.

"Here's Anthony now," Donovan said, turning me toward him.

I turned around and my mouth dropped open. I could not believe what I was seeing.

"Vic?" I said as I stared at Camille's boyfriend.

"Oh, I thought you hadn't met him," Donovan said, confused.

I folded my arms, attitude all over my face. "I hadn't met *Anthony*, but I have met *Vic*." It was all adding up now. No wonder Camille and Alexis couldn't get their boyfriends together. He was the same guy!

"Is your girl here yet?" Donovan asked.

I looked at Vic with gritted teeth to see how he was going to answer that and which girlfriend he was referring to.

"Ummm, Alexis will be here in a minute," he said, shifting nervously.

I just continued staring at him. I could not believe Camille and Alexis were dating the same guy.

"So, what's your name?" I said. "Is it Anthony or Vic?"

Donovan looked at me strangely.

At first, Anthony, Vic, whatever his name was, looked uncomfortable, but that cockiness of his quickly returned. "It's Anthony Vickers. Some people call me Vic."

"Umph, do they now?" I wasn't sure if I should bust him right then or what. I was just about to say something when Alexis came bouncing up. She threw her arms around Anthony.

"Hey, baby," she said, kissing him on the lips.

She turned to me. "What's up, Jasmine? I see you finally met my boo." She then turned to Donovan, a surprised look on her face. "Hey, Donovan. I didn't know you'd be here. How's school going?"

"What's up, girl? Long time no see."

Donovan hugged her while Anthony glared at me over her shoulder. I could not believe this fool was trying to play my friends. I knew I had to ask Alexis to come to the bathroom with me so I could tell her what was going on. Anthony must've suspected what I was about to do because he quickly spoke to Donovan.

"Yo, man, I know it's been a while since you've seen Jasmine. The teams are still warming up—why don't you take her outside and spend some quality time with her?"

Donovan looked at him strangely. But something must have been in his eyes, because Donovan responded, "Yeah, I think that's a good idea."

As bad as I wanted to blow up Anthony's spot right then and there, the prospect of spending time with Donovan was definitely more appealing. I looked in Donovan's eyes and decided Anthony could wait a few minutes.

Alexis giggled as Donovan took my hand and led me outside. "Don't do anything I wouldn't do," she called out after me.

"What's that all about?" Donovan said as we sat down on a bench outside.

"Your boy is not only going with Alexis, he's going with Camille, too." I didn't try to hide the fact that I didn't appreciate that.

"What? Your other friend, Camille?"

"Yeah," I replied. "Only Camille knows him as Vic. That's what I met him as when I was with her."

"Dang," Donovan said. He was actually smiling, like Anthony should've been given props or something. "I mean, I can't believe he's doing that," he backpedaled when he noticed the upset look on my face. "I'm just trippin' because of all the girls in Houston, Anthony gon' go and hook up with two best friends."

"Yeah, my point exactly. But he won't be hooked up after tonight."

"Why do you say that?"

"Because I'm going to tell Alexis," I replied. That was a no-brainer.

"Maybe you should just stay out of it," he softly suggested.

"Stay out of it?" I looked at him like he had lost his mind. "Those are my friends. I can't stay out of it."

Donovan shrugged. "I'm just saying, I'm sure he didn't know Alexis and Camille were friends. Let me talk to him first and find out the real deal. Alexis looks like she's really feeling him; maybe he'll come clean with her. It would be a whole lot better coming from him than you. We'll just go back in and enjoy the game. I'll talk to him after the game and maybe I can tell you what he said tomorrow when I take you out to dinner."

Suddenly, all I heard was the dinner part. I smiled again. I knew I probably shouldn't be giving Donovan the time of day the way he just dumped me when he went off to college, but I couldn't help it. The next thing I knew, I was saying, "All right, but he better tell her tonight or I'm telling her tomorrow."

"Right, right," Donovan said, scooting closer to me. "Now, can we talk about what I really wanted to talk to you about?"

"What's that?" I said.

"This," he said, moving in and planting a deep kiss smack dead on my lips. And Alexis, Camille, and their shared boyfriend quickly disappeared from my mind. All I could think about was how nobody had ever made me feel quite like Donovan did.

10

Jasmine

I was back to reality now. I'd spent all night dreaming about the kiss from Donovan. But now, after lying around the house most of the day, my mind had returned to how Anthony was trying to play two of my best friends.

Despite what Donovan said, I had the strangest feeling that I was going to have to be the one to break the news. Somehow I just didn't see Anthony coming clean.

"Why are you on my bed?" I said as I walked into my bedroom and saw my older sister stretched out, polishing her nails. Since we'd moved into a bigger apartment, I no longer had to share a room with my grandmother, who snored so loud it rocked the pictures off the walls. But I did have to share the small room with Nikki. I thought that since she was eighteen she'd have been long gone by now, but she was still here. And even though she'd graduated, she had no plans to go to college and was content with her job at the beauty supply store. I think she was hoping her boyfriend, Tony, would get drafted by the NBA and marry her, and then she'd live large as a baller's wife. But so far, he was just playing at the community college outside of Dallas because he barely passed the college entrance exams.

"I made my bed up earlier. You hadn't. So since yours was already messed up, I figured what was the harm," she replied nonchalantly as she polished her fingernails a bright blue.

"The harm is I don't want you on my bed," I said, picking up her stuffed teddy bear and throwing it at her.

She moved just as the bear was about to collide with her head. "Why are you in such a funk all the time lately? Dang."

"Just get off my bed."

"Whatever." She groaned and blew on her fingernails. My sister and I didn't have the best of relationships but every now and then she did have some good advice. I finally decided maybe I should ask her what I should do about Camille and Alexis.

"Look, I'm sorry for snapping at you. I'm just stressin'."

"What you got to be stressed about?"

I sighed as I sat down on her bed and kicked off my tennis shoes.

"Okay. You know Camille and Alexis, right?"

"Yeah, your friends from that booty-butt group you're in."

I rolled my eyes and tried not to let her get under my skin. "I found out last night that Camille and Alexis are dating the same guy."

"Whaaat?" Nikki said. She always did love gossip. She screwed the top on the polish and looked my way. "You for real?"

"Yeah. He's messing with both of them."

"Well, did he know they were friends?"

"What difference does that make?"

"A lot, because if he did know, he's just low-down. If he didn't know, he's just being a dude," Nikki said like she was an expert on relationships.

"Well, I don't know whether he knew in the beginning or not, but after I busted him, he still tried to act all hard when I said something to him about it. But here's the deal: He's a friend of Donovan's."

"Ooooh, the cutie-pie?" Nikki grinned. "What's he up to?"

I groaned. "Can you stay focused, please?"

"Umpph, I just can't figure out how you let that one get away."

"Forget it," I said, standing up.

"A'ight." She sat up and gave me her full attention. "Finish telling me."

"Donovan said he was going to talk to Anthony, but

somehow I have the feeling that he's not, or if he does, it won't even matter. I mean, that is his boy and all. So I'm trying to see if I should tell them."

I could tell my sister liked me coming to her for advice. She tossed her fire red braids over her shoulder, looking like she was deep in thought. "You know, personally I would stay out of it."

That definitely was not what I expected her to say. "You're kidding, right?"

"No, seriously. Both of them are really feelin' this guy, right?"

"Yeah."

"Well, I'ma tell you what I know. In cases like this, it's the messenger who ends up getting hurt the most."

I shot her a confused look. My sister had mastered ebonics, so the fact that she wasn't breaking this down in her usual ghetto fashion was confusing. "What does that mean?"

She sighed and spoke slowly, as if talking to a child. "What are you gonna do if you tell them and they don't believe you? Or worse, they think you're just hatin' 'cause you ain't got no man?"

"That's stupid. Why would they not believe me? They're my best friends."

"And? When it comes to love, friendship takes a backseat," she said matter-of-factly.

That shut me up. "Who died and made you Dr. Phil?" I finally asked.

She shrugged. "I'm just tellin' you. You being the one to tell them is just gon' create more mess."

I shook my head. "I see it creating more mess if I *don't* tell them. I, for one, know that if either one of them knew something like this and didn't tell me, it would be on."

Nikki crossed her legs and leaned back. "Okay, say they do believe you, but they choose to stay with him anyway—"

"How they gon' stay with him?" I said, cutting her off. "They wouldn't stay with him."

"Do you know that for a fact?"

I just stared at her. Of course I knew that. Or at least I thought I did.

"Think about it. Both of them are head over heels in love with this guy. Who's to say he won't give them some excuse and they stay anyway? And he'll make *you* out to look like some loser who's just jealous."

I thought about what she was saying. "Naw, once they find out, they will definitely kick him to the curb."

"I've seen this situation too many times and that's not how it usually happens. You remember Dana from next door in the old apartment?" She didn't give me time to answer. "Same situation. Her best friend tried to tell her something about her boyfriend and Dana ended up hating her friend and staying with her trifling boyfriend. It didn't take long for her to finally see that dog for his true colors, but she destroyed a friendship behind that mess. So you should just stay out of it. They'll see for themselves soon enough that he ain't no good."

I was dumbfounded. "So you don't think I should say anything for real?"

She looked at me, irritated. "I said no. I think you're going to regret it if you do."

"But, I just don't think . . ."

"Look, you asked for my opinion. My opinion is keep your mouth shut." She stretched back out across my bed, opened up her *VIBE* magazine, and began reading. Her body language told me she was done talking. And I was more confused than ever.

11

Jasmine

I felt sick to my stomach.

I mean, it's like Anthony just thought he was so big and bad that he could ignore my threats. I couldn't believe his arrogance as he put his arm around Camille when they walked toward where I stood outside the gate after school. Maybe he thought Donovan had me so wrapped up that I wouldn't tell. Well, if he did think that, this fool was dumber than he looked.

"Hey, Jas," Camille said, "look who surprised me and popped up outside my last class." She grinned at Anthony. She must not have noticed the look of disgust on my face because she kept grinning like she was retarded or something.

"What's up, Jas?" Anthony said, like we were the best of friends.

I didn't bother responding to him. Instead, I looked at Camille. "I need to talk to you for a minute." I glanced at Anthony. "Privately." Obviously, he hadn't said a word. He probably hadn't ever planned to. I'd called Donovan to ask him about it yesterday. He said he hadn't had a chance to talk to Anthony yet. But he agreed with my sister that I should just stay out of it. Well, I had news for him *and* my sister: I wasn't staying out of it. I was about to tell Camille the real deal right now.

Anthony kept that cocky smile, but quickly said to Camille, "Babe, can you believe I left my backpack by your locker? Do you mind running and getting it for me before they lock up the building?"

Camille kept grinning. "Sure, baby."

"Camille," I said with more force in my voice, "I need to talk to you."

"Gimme a minute. I'll be right back," she said as she darted off.

As soon as she walked into the building, Anthony turned to me scowling. "What do you want to talk to my girl about?"

I bucked up to him, giving him a look to let him know that he didn't scare me. "Not that it's any of your business, but I want to talk to her about your *other* girl. You know, her best friend, the one that you're cheating on her with. I guess you thought I was playin' with you when I said you'd better tell her or I would."

Anthony backed up and laughed. "Naw, I just didn't think you'd be stupid enough to let Donovan go over this little misunderstanding."

"Man, Donovan is already gone." Sure, he had me all floating the other day when he kissed me, but I wasn't stupid. When he got back to college, I'd be history again, no matter what he said. "I don't know what kind of game you and Donovan are runnin', but it ain't gonna work."

"Go ahead and tell. They feelin' me so much, it's no biggie. I'll just say you want me, too, which you probably do."

I stared at him. *Fool, please.* He looked good and all, but I couldn't understand how he could be so arrogant, acting like what he was doing was no big deal. What made him think he could play two girls, best friends at that? And to think I thought he was one of the good guys.

Anthony leaned in to me and whispered, "You can tell either one of them right now, but I bet you by next week, we'll be back to kickin' it."

I looked at him like he was crazy. That was the same nonsense Nikki was talking. But no way could my friends be that dumb. "I guess we'll just have to see about that."

"I guess we will," he replied, backing up just as Camille came.

"Vic, baby, I didn't see your backpack. Are you sure you brought it in? I don't remember you having it."

He snapped his fingers. "Dang, you're right. I left it in Montrell's car when he dropped me off. Oh, well—sorry to make you run back inside for nothing."

He leaned in and kissed her. She giggled like a seventh grader. I wanted to throw up.

"Well, I better get going," Anthony said. "I told Montrell I'd meet him down the street at four and it's five after now. Besides, I know Jasmine wants to talk to you." He sneered at me. "Maybe she wants to tell you all about Donovan wanting to get back with her."

"What?" Camille said. "You didn't tell me that."

I rolled my eyes. Anthony laughed as he walked off. He took a couple of steps, then turned back to Camille. "Oh, yeah, Camille?"

"Yeah?" she said.

"I love you." With that he turned and continued on down the street.

Camille looked like she was about to pass out. "I love you, too," she called out after him. I couldn't believe this fool. He was straight trippin'. Well, I hated to be the one to bust Camille's little happy bubble, but Anthony had left me no choice.

"Camille, I really need to—" I stopped talking when Mrs. McNeil, Camille's drill team coach, walked up.

"Miss Harris, did you forget about our mandatory drill team meeting this afternoon?"

Camille slapped her forehead. "Oh, snap. I did."

"Well, let's get moving. They've already started." Mrs. McNeil stood waiting on Camille.

"Sorry, Jas," she told me. "I'll have to catch up with you tonight at the meeting. I gotta go."

She took off with Mrs. McNeil before I could utter another word.

12

Jasmine

Angel and I stood outside the meeting room. I had filled her in on everything. She was just as shocked as I was that Anthony was trying to play Camille and Alexis and agreed that we needed to tell them both, no matter how they reacted.

"As soon as they get here, we'll tell them the truth," Angel said.

"I agree. I know they're really feelin' this guy, but he is low-down," I added.

Camille walked in just as Alexis came bouncing up in her usual chipper mood. "Hey, hey, hey," she said. "Now what's so important that you guys have us coming early?"

Angel looked at me and I took a deep breath. "Look, I

don't know any other way to say this than to come right out and say it. Alexis and Camille, your boyfriend is a dog."

The smile immediately left both of their faces.

"Excuse me?" Alexis said.

"Just what I said," I replied. I probably should've been a little more gentle, but tact never was one of my strong points.

"What are you talking about?" Camille asked.

"Yeah," Alexis echoed. "You've only met Anthony one time so how can you say that?"

"No, actually, I've met him quite a few times—with Camille."

Camille scrunched up her nose. "What? I've never even seen Alexis's man, so how can you say you met him with me?"

I inhaled, and glanced at Angel. She gave me an encouraging nod. "Yes, Camille. You've met him. Several times. Only you know him as Vic."

They both shot me confused looks as I continued. "His real name is Anthony Vickers but he also goes by the nickname Vic."

"This must be some mistake," Alexis said.

I sighed. "No mistake. When I met him at the basketball game the other night, I called him out about it."

"Are you trying to tell me that me and Alexis are dating the same guy?" Camille asked.

I nodded. Suddenly Camille started laughing. "Girl,

you are so stupid. What kind of joke is this? You aren't even funny."

"I wish I was joking." I looked at Angel. "Tell them, Angel."

Angel stepped forward, a sad look across her face. "She's telling the truth. Anthony has been playing both of you."

I finally told them all about me bumping into Anthony at the basketball game. I also told them how cocky he was, even after finding out they were best friends.

"Why didn't you say anything to me that night?" Alexis asked when I finished.

"I think I was just in shock. I was trying to figure out what was going on. I didn't want to come to you guys without knowing the whole story."

Camille looked at me. I could tell she was getting upset. "Well, what story is there to know? If he's dating both of us, then that's the end of the story."

"I don't know." I felt myself getting defensive. I knew I should've said something right away. "For all I know he could've had a twin or something."

"I don't believe this," Camille said. "This fool was playing me?"

Alexis looked at her. "Playing us." She turned her attention back to me. "What I'm not understanding is, that basketball game was a week ago. Why are you just now saying something?"

"I was trying to give him the opportunity to tell you

guys because I didn't want no drama, I didn't want it coming from me," I said.

"And why not? Especially if you're supposed to be our best friend," Camille snapped.

"Look, I was just trying to do the right thing. He said he was going to tell you. I thought maybe he didn't realize the two of you were friends."

"He couldn't have known that we were friends," Alexis said.

"Oh, maybe he didn't at first, but after he saw me at the game he knew," I said. "And he had the nerve to tell me y'all both were so into him that it wouldn't matter. He said even if you did break up with him, he could get you back within a week."

"Oh, did he say that?" Camille said. She was furious. Her eyebrows were pinched together, her fists were balled up, and she was pacing back and forth. Alexis, on the other hand, simply looked shocked. She stood there shaking her head like she couldn't believe it.

"Oh, this fool done lost his mind," Camille snapped.

"My point exactly," I replied. "I mean, it's one thing if he thought he was just playing two different girls, but to try and play best friends, that's low."

"And he got me jumped behind his cheating butt. Oh no, it's about to be on." She pulled out her cell phone.

Alexis grabbed her arm. "Wait a minute, Camille. We need to think this through."

"Think what through? Ain't nothing to think through. I'm about to give him a piece of my mind."

"And what is that going to accomplish?" Alexis said.

Camille snapped her phone shut. "And why are you taking up for him?"

"I'm not taking up for him. I'm just as mad as you are," Alexis replied. "But we need to come up with a plan."

"A plan?" Camille and I said at the same time.

Angel smiled. "I'm feeling you, Alexis. Don't just call and curse him out because he'll just hang up and block your number. You need to bust him in a way he'll never forget."

Alexis finally smiled. "Exactly—and I've got the perfect plan."

13

Jasmine

It was a perfect day for a beach party. The sun was shining brightly and there wasn't a cloud in sight. At first, I was worried about a beach party in September, but this is Texas, so I guess I should've known it would still be hot. The good thing was it wasn't so hot that we'd burn up; just hot enough to sport the cutest swimsuits.

Myself, I had on a royal blue one-piece that tied around the neck and a pair of long shorts. I just couldn't do the Daisy Dukes like Camille wanted me to. Angel was dressed pretty conservative like me. Alexis and Camille, however, both wore bikinis and some dainty little skirts. I guess they had to look their sexiest for the big payback.

"Okay, girls, are we ready for Operation Make Anthony Sweat?" Alexis said. That girl was on a mission. I don't think I'd ever seen her with such a determined attitude. No doubt, finding out about Anthony had ticked her off and she seemed bent on making him pay.

We were in Alexis's car heading down Highway 45 toward Galveston. The beach party was being sponsored by a local college fraternity and was all anyone had been talking about for weeks.

"Operation Make Anthony Sweat?" I laughed. "Do you come up with this corny stuff on your own or do you get help from somewhere?"

"Whatever. You're just mad because you didn't think of it," Alexis joked.

I shook my head as we continued to laugh and talk during the ride.

"I can't wait to see the look on Vic's face when we bust him," Camille said, as she lowered the sun visor and checked her makeup.

"Are you sure he's gonna be there?" Angel said.

"Yep, he'll be there," Alexis said. "He doesn't think I will, though. I told him I had something to do."

"And he thinks I'm just swinging through," Camille added.

"Donovan is his boy. You don't think he'll say something?" Angel asked.

I tried not to think about Donovan. He'd returned to school last week and, as expected, I hadn't heard from him since.

"Donovan is back in Austin and they've started basketball practice. I doubt seriously if he'll even be here," I said.

It took us almost forty-five minutes to get to Galveston and another twenty minutes to navigate through all the traffic along the beachfront. We finally found where most of the high schoolers were hanging out. This was a college-sponsored event but, of course, the younger crowd came out in full force.

"Now, do we need to review the plan again?" Alexis said.

"Girl, please," I snapped. "We've reviewed the plan a hundred times. You act like we're on a top-secret mission or something."

"I just want to make sure we don't mess this up," Alexis replied.

"Chill," Camille said, checking her makeup yet again. "Everything will be fine. Just drop me off, then go find a place to park."

"Won't he wonder what you're doing here alone?" Angel asked.

Alexis exhaled in frustration. "See, this is why we needed to review the plan."

I rolled my eyes. They were about to get on my nerves.

"Angel," Alexis said. "We've already said that Camille will tell him she's here with some of the girls from the drill team."

"Oh, yeah," Angel said. "I forgot."

Alexis pulled off to the side to let Camille out. "Okay, let's put this plan into action."

Camille smiled as she stepped out of the car. I had to admit, my girl was looking good. She had her hair down and curly, held out of her face by a pair of Gucci sunglasses (of course, they were Alexis's). She was sporting a black-and-gold bikini top; the bottoms peeked out from under her low-rise mini. A pair of strappy gold sandals set the outfit off.

We drove around for fifteen minutes as planned. After that, Alexis pulled out her cell phone and called Camille.

"Did you find him yet?" She pushed the button to put Camille on the speakerphone.

"Yeah," Camille said. "Hold on." We heard some muffled conversation, then silence. Then she said, "Okay, I told Vic I was trying to tell my friends where I was, so I'm sitting in one of his boys' car. We're by the lighthouse."

"Okay, we're heading that way."

We parked on the south beach, close enough to the lighthouse so that we could see, but far enough not to get noticed by Anthony.

We watched Camille do her thang. Anthony was all over her and she was flirting something crazy. Alexis sent Camille a text message—the signal for her to disappear for a minute so Anthony would answer his cell phone.

"Next phase of the plan," Alexis said, dialing Anthony's number. "Now, let's just hope he answers."

"Hey, Anthony, baby." Alexis smiled at us. We were worried that he wouldn't answer when he saw Alexis's number. But we were hoping that with Camille all of a sudden having to go to the restroom he'd pick up. Thank goodness he did. "Whatcha doing?" Alexis asked.

"Put him on speakerphone so we can hear what he's saying," I whispered to Alexis.

She shushed me, but pushed the speaker button.

" . . . so, we're not really doin' anything. Just hanging out. It's kinda boring. They didn't have a really good turnout, so me and my boys 'bout to roll back to Houston," Anthony said.

I looked at all the people gathered on the beach. "Liar," I mouthed.

Alexis rolled her eyes, but quickly returned to her conversation. "Oh really? It looks like there are quite a few people here to me."

Anthony was quiet for a minute. Me, Alexis, and Angel fought back a laugh.

"Y-you're here?" he stammered.

"Yeah, that's what I was calling you for. I got done early so I decided to come down with some of the girls from my school."

"Oh." He sounded shocked.

"Where are you? I wanna come see you," Alexis purred. "I want you to see how cute I look in my swimsuit."

"Ummmm, well, me and my boys, we . . . we were about to go."

"Can't you get them to wait a few minutes?"

"Naw, they're really ready to go," he said. "Why don't I just give you a call later on today. Maybe I can swing by your crib and take you out to eat or something."

Alexis twisted her lips as she looked at us and shook her head. "Well, I'm already on the beach. I can still see you before you go. By the time you make it through all the traffic, I could've been to you."

I pulled Alexis's arm and pointed toward Camille, who was walking back toward Anthony. Anthony looked up and saw her.

"Well, I gotta go," Anthony quickly said. "I can hardly hear you with all this noise."

"Anthony!" Alexis shouted. "Where are you? I'm on the beach already. I can be there in five minutes."

"Ummm, okay. I'm on north beach. Come on down. I'll wait on you." He slammed the phone shut before she could say another word.

Alexis snapped her cell phone shut and threw it into her bag. "He is such a freakin' liar. Talkin' about ain't nobody here. It's twelve gazillion people here. And then gon' tell me he's on the *north* beach."

"That's because while you're looking for him on the north beach, he's gonna be hightailing it off the south beach," I said, even more disgusted with his lying behind.

"Yeah," Angel added. "Then he's probably gonna give you some excuse about how he waited for you."

"And I'd be willing to bet if you called him back, he wouldn't answer his phone," I said.

"Well, I got something for him all right," Alexis said, opening her car door and stepping out of the car. "Let's go."

It only took us a few minutes to get to where Anthony

and his friends were. He looked like he was trying to convince Camille of something. We walked up behind him just as Camille said, "But I'm not ready to go."

"North beach, huh?" Alexis said, her arms folded across her chest.

Anthony spun around.

"What's up, Anthony? Or should I say, Vic?" Alexis spat.

Anthony's eyes popped open wide. "A-Alexis?"

"In the flesh." She twisted up her lips. "I'm gonna ask you again: What's up?"

"N-nothing," he said, looking back and forth between her and Camille. By this time, the group of people around us knew something was about to go down, and everybody started turning their attention toward us.

"Oh, so now I'm nothing?" Camille said, getting an attitude herself. Our plan was coming together well.

"Ain't nobody talking to you," Alexis replied, pointing a finger in Camille's face. "You supposed to be my friend and you down here messing with my man?"

Camille stepped into Alexis's face. "Excuse me, but last I checked, he was my man."

Alexis bucked up to her, balling up her fist. "You need to get your funky breath out of my face before I stomp you in this beach sand."

I fought back a laugh. Was that supposed to be her tough-girl role? *Stomp you in this beach sand?* Alexis couldn't come up with nothing better than that?

"Bring it," Camille said, wiggling her neck.

Alexis stepped back. "You ain't even worth me getting my nails dirty." She looked at Anthony. "Who is it gon' be? Me or her?"

Camille turned to Anthony as well. "Yeah, Vic. Me or her?"

By this point, Anthony was sweating like crazy. The crowd behind him was laughing and taking pictures with their camera phones. They were definitely enjoying the show.

"C-can we go somewhere and talk about this?" Anthony said.

"Naw, we want an answer now!" Camille demanded.

He looked back and forth between the two of them. This was the part of the plan that had me worried. I was concerned that if he actually did choose one of them, the other one would get mad. But both Camille and Alexis had promised that they wouldn't.

"Take the Beyoncé-lookin' one," some boy screamed from the side.

"Uh-uh, take the fine brown-skinned thing. Lawd, have mercy," another boy countered.

Anthony trembled as he continued to look back and forth. "It's not even like that . . ."

"Choose!" Alexis yelled.

"Okay, okay." He rubbed his head. "Alexis, I'm sorry. But I really wanna be with Camille," he stammered. A mixture of boos and cheers came from the crowd.

I could've sworn I saw a flicker of pain in Alexis's eyes, but she quickly covered by trying to look mad.

Camille, on the other hand, smiled triumphantly.

"Camille, come here, boo. I didn't mean for it to all come out like this," he said.

Camille sashayed over to him. A relieved grin spread across his face. "I'm so glad you're not mad at me. I was—"

Camille took her hand and pushed Anthony's forehead back as hard as she could. "Fool, please."

Anthony caught himself from falling and looked at Camille, stunned.

"Do you think I really want your low-down, dirty butt?" She pointed to Alexis. "That's my best friend. And you gon' try to run game on *us*? I don't think so. Neither one of us wants your janky, lying, fake-Omarion, triflin' behind."

"Oooooh, I guess she told you," some girl from the crowd yelled.

"Tell that dog where to go!" another girl shouted.

Alexis moved up next to Camille. "Newsflash, bruh, you ain't got it like that. See ya, wouldn't want to be ya!"

She flicked him off, then swung her hair in his face as she turned around and strutted off.

Camille laughed at him one last time. "You're just sorry." She sashayed off as well. Me and Angel followed. I made sure I turned and shot him a satisfied smile. He was still standing there, dumbfounded, as the crowd continued to laugh and point at him.

We were in the car and pulling out of the beach parking lot when all of us busted out laughing.

"That was so off the chain," Angel said.

"It was, wasn't it?" Alexis replied as she gave Camille a high five.

I leaned up in the seat, still giggling. "Just one thing, Alexis."

"What?" she said, eyeing me in the rearview mirror.

" 'Stomp you in this beach sand'? 'See ya, wouldn't want to be ya'? Girl, you need to come hang out in the hood a little bit more!"

We all laughed as we made our way back to Houston. Operation Make Anthony Sweat was a resounding success.

14

Angel

I couldn't believe my eyes. I stood outside Alexis's house watching with my jaw on the ground. I just knew I wasn't seeing what I thought I was seeing.

What happened to our plan? What happened to everything we said? Everything we did? Was it all for nothing?

Because here Alexis was, standing in front of her house—with Anthony. The beach party was less than a week ago and she had that fool all up in her face.

It wouldn't have been so bad if she was going off on him or something, but she was grinning at him like he was Chris Brown or something.

I walked up to her and loudly cleared my throat. I

didn't even try to hide the attitude across my face. "What's goin' on, Alexis?"

Alexis jumped back when she saw me. "Oh. Hey, Angel," she said, nervously. "I wasn't expecting you so soon."

"Obviously," I replied, cutting my eyes at Anthony. "My sister was headed this way, so I just had her drop me off. What's going on?"

Anthony smiled and said, "What's up, Angel?"

I ignored him and turned back to Alexis. "Camille," I said, stressing her name, "is gonna meet us here before we go to the community service project." We were going for our monthly visit at the Julia C. Hester House, a senior citizens' center.

"Cool," Alexis said, still looking all nervous. I definitely wanted to hear how she planned to explain this.

"Well, I'm gonna let you girls do your thing." Anthony chuckled. He leaned in and kissed Alexis on the lips. "I'll call you later, baby girl."

I stood there waiting for her to haul off and smack him upside the head or something, but instead she just said, "Okay."

"Later, Angel," he said, as he strutted down the circular driveway toward his mustard-colored truck.

"You want to tell me what is going on?" I said as soon as he got in his truck.

"Nothing's going on," she said, turning and walking into her house.

I followed close on her heels. "That wasn't 'nothing' I

just saw. Did you get back with him?" I knew that couldn't possibly be it, but I was struggling to make sense of why she was even giving him the time of day. "Alexis, answer me," I demanded as I walked up the spiral staircase behind her.

We were inside her room before she turned and answered me. "Angel, I'm cool, okay? Let me handle this."

"How can you get back with him?" I asked in disbelief.

Alexis sighed as she sat down to log on to her laptop. "You don't understand."

I stood in front of her, my arms crossed. "What's to understand?"

"Hey, what's up?" We both turned toward Jasmine, who was standing in the door. "I called out to you guys when I was coming up the sidewalk. Y'all just came on inside. Sonja let me in. What are you two talking about that you don't even hear me yelling your names?"

I didn't take my eyes off of Alexis. "You don't even wanna know."

Jasmine got that this was serious because she didn't say anything smart. She just stomped over to us and said, "Somebody better tell me what's going on."

Alexis rolled her eyes but didn't answer. So I turned to Jasmine and said, "I guess Anthony was right about Alexis not caring that he was dating her and Camille."

"What?" Jasmine proclaimed. "What does that mean?"

"It means she got back together with him."

Jasmine leaned in and stared at Alexis. "Please tell me she's lying."

"Lying about what?" Camille said, smiling as she walked into the room. She plopped down on the bed. "Sonja let me in. What is Alexis lying about?" When no one responded, the smile left her face. "Okay, what's up? Why are you guys standing around looking like you're mad at the world?"

I stared at Alexis. I didn't want to just call her out like that but I was mad and I knew Jasmine was, too.

"Yeah, Alexis, you want to tell her what's going on?" Jasmine snapped.

Alexis rolled her eyes and let out a deep breath. "Not like it's anybody's business, but me and Anthony got back together."

Camille's mouth dropped open. "Excuse me? I know I must've heard you wrong."

Alexis looked up defiantly. "You heard me. We're back together."

Camille crossed her arms and narrowed her eyes. "And why would you do a stupid thing like that?"

Alexis seemed to soften her defiant stance. "Look, I'm going to need you guys to just trust me, all right? I know what I'm doing. I'm not stupid."

"No, you are a genius for giving this cheating fool another chance," Jasmine said sarcastically. "Do I need to remind you that he played you *and* one of your best friends?"

"You don't need to remind me of anything," Alexis said.

"Come on, Alexis, get real here," I added, trying to keep my tone reasonable.

"No, you guys get real. I was really feeling Anthony and

everybody makes mistakes." Alexis didn't sound the least bit convinced.

Jasmine laughed. "Mistake? Is that what you call it?"

"Okay, let me explain to you all. I know what it looks like, but really—," Alexis began.

"I don't believe this," Camille said, cutting her off.

"For real, though, just listen—"

"Oh no you didn't." Camille immediately started going off as she stood back up and towered over Alexis, who was still sitting at her desk. "Anthony tried to play both of us. We came up with this elaborate plan to bust him—*your* plan at that—and you're going to sit here and stab me in the back? I mean, I was feelin' him just like you, but the bottom line for me was I valued our friendship too much. You obviously don't feel the same way."

Alexis sat quietly as Camille continued to go off.

"You know what? Why does this not surprise me about your bougie behind? You think you're all that. Just because you have money you think you can get whatever you want and you don't care who you hurt."

Alexis's eyes were watering up but she didn't say anything.

"I always knew there was something about you that I didn't like anyway," Camille continued. "And now I know what it is. It's because you ain't nothing but a backstabbing, lying skank! You and Anthony deserve each other. I'm out." She turned and stormed out of the room. I don't think I'd ever seen Camille that mad.

Both me and Jasmine stared at Alexis. Her chest was

heaving up and down. I couldn't tell if she was fighting back tears, anger, or both. I don't know about Jasmine, but I really didn't know what to say to Alexis. I was so disappointed. Jasmine was obviously still mad because she just shook her head as she followed Camille out of the room.

"Alexis, you're buggin' out," I said, following everybody out. I couldn't believe it. Once again, our friendship was falling apart. And this time, I didn't see any way it could be saved.

15

Jasmine

I stared at Camille. She was giggling as she stuffed a corn dog bite into her mouth. It was a beautiful and breezy day as we sat on the patio at the James Coney Island restaurant. She was laughing about something nobody else found funny.

"So how long are we just going to pretend that everything is fine? How long are we going to stay mad at Alexis?" I asked. It had been three days and neither Camille nor Alexis had made a move to patch things up. Me and Angel spent the first couple of days just as mad as Camille, but now we both felt it was time to deal with this.

"Who?" Camille asked, trying to look like she really didn't know who I was talking about.

I clicked my teeth. "You know, your best friend, Alexis?"

"You mean my *former* best friend."

"Come on, Camille. Don't you think we need to at least hear her out?" I had spent a lot of time trying to sort all of this out and I'd just come to the conclusion that Alexis had to have a really good reason for getting back together with Anthony—although for the life of me, I couldn't figure out what it was. But that was the only thing I could think of that would explain this.

"What's there to hear?" Camille nonchalantly said as she slurped her soda. "She chose her side. So I don't have anything to say to her. It's bad enough I have to watch out for these other tricks trying to take my man; now I gotta worry about my own friends? Bump that."

"So what are we gonna do?" Angel asked.

"I don't know what *y'all* gon' do, but me, I let those other girls slide when they jumped me. I'm not about to let someone else, especially a so-called friend, make a fool out of me."

Angel leaned in and looked Camille in the eye. "What does that mean?"

"It means what it means," Camille said, rolling her neck. I could tell that look in her eyes wasn't good.

"Camille, what are you planning?" Angel asked.

"I'm planning payback. Alexis doesn't know who she's messing with." She sipped her drink again. "But I'm about to show her."

"Th-this doesn't sound good," Angel stuttered.

"That's 'cause it ain't. You remember when we were looking at getting those girls that jumped me. Well, since Keysha is crazy I think I need to drop a little bug in her ear about Alexis. Maybe even make her think Anthony was going to get back with her until Alexis talked him out of it. And I'm going to make sure she gets this." She pulled a folded-up piece of paper out of her purse and slid it across the table. I was the first to take it. I opened it. My eyes grew wide as I read it.

"Read it out loud," Angel said.

I shook my head. " 'Dear Keysha, I'm a good friend of Anthony and therefore I want to see him happy. I know that he was happiest when he was with you. I was talking to him last week and he told me he was going to beg you to take him back. But then, this girl he was seeing named Alexis (she's a rich girl from St. Pius High School) talked him out of it. She told him that you were a nasty tramp that had slept with several guys on the football team.' Oh, my God," I said, stopping and looking up at Camille, who had a smug look on her face. "I can not believe you're gonna do this."

"I told you, Alexis doesn't know who she's messing with."

Angel's mouth remained open as I continued reading.

" 'Alexis thinks she's all that, just because her parents have money. She thinks she can buy whatever and whoever she wants. She told Anthony that he would be happier with her and all the things she could do for him, and said your mama is on welfare so why would he want to be with

you. Alexis drives a blue BMW and she's always over Anthony's house. I ain't trying to be in your business, but I
just thought that you should know. Signed, a friend.' "

I looked up at Camille. "Have you lost your mind?"

"Nope."

"Camille," Angel said. "You can't give her that."

"Watch me." Camille flashed a wicked smile. "I told
you, payback ain't no joke. And Alexis is about to find that
out firsthand."

The evil look in Camille's eyes made me shiver. I'd
never seen her look like that. And I had a terrible feeling
that things among the Good Girlz were going to get a
whole lot worse before they got better.

16

Angel

"Angel, pay attention, *por favor!*"

My mother's voice snapped me out of the trance I'd been drifting in for the past few hours.

"Are you even watching my granddaughter?" She pointed to Angelica, who had found a half-empty Coke can and emptied it all over herself trying to drink it. "*¡Ella lo hace mal!*"

My mother raced over, took the can away, and began trying to clean Angelica up. Angelica found the whole scene funny and was giggling like crazy.

"Where is your mind, *niña?*" my mother chastised.

I was lying across the floor in the living room. Angelica had been crawling around playing with her building blocks. Usually, I got the greatest joy watching my baby, but today, my mind couldn't focus on much of anything except what was going on with my friends.

I actually didn't have any real close friends until the Good Girlz. I was sort of a loner, a quiet and shy girl until I hooked up with them. They'd brought me out of my shell and we'd created a bond that was very special to me. That's why all of this stuff we were going through was stressing me out.

I couldn't believe my friends had reached this point. I couldn't believe that Camille was even considering doing something as foul as siccing Keysha on Alexis.

"I have to get to work," my mother said as she pulled off Angelica's wet top. "Watch your child, *por favor?*"

"Yeah, yeah, yeah," I said, as I stood up and took Angelica from her. "I hear you. I just have a lot on my mind."

My mother squeezed my chin. "I know. And I wish that you'd talk to me."

I forced a smile. "It's nothing major. Go on before you're late for work." I kissed her and used my free hand to shoo her out the door to her job as a librarian with the Houston Public Library.

She was barely out of the door before my older sister, Rosita, who had been taking a nap in the back, walked into the room. "What was mami in here fussing about?"

"Nothin'," I replied. "Just on my case because Angelica spilled a soda."

Rosita yawned and plopped down on the sofa. "Shoot, she was about to wake up the kids. Thank goodness she didn't." My sister had three kids and I knew she had a hard time raising them by herself, which is why she was always over my mom's, even though she had a small two-bedroom house.

"Okay, what's got you so down in the dumps?" Rosita said, finally noticing the sad look on my face.

As much as I wanted to talk about it, my sister had enough problems with her children's deadbeat dad. She hadn't seen her ex-husband since her youngest was four months old, and that was three years ago. So she was struggling financially and constantly stressed out. Not to mention the losers she was always dating.

"Look, I've been around you all sixteen years of your life and trust me, I can tell when something is wrong," Rosita said.

I sat Angelica down and she immediately took off back toward the blocks.

"Let me guess," Rosita continued. "This has something to do with Marcus, right?"

I cut my eyes at her. How come whenever you get down about something, people always assume it's behind a boy?

"No, it's not about Marcus," I replied. I didn't care if I never talked to him again. I hated that he refused to develop a relationship with his daughter, but that was between him and God. I'd done my part to try and get him to do right.

"It's my friends. You know, the ones in that church group with me?"

Rosita nodded. "Yeah, I really like those girls. And that group."

I sighed. "Yeah, me too. But we're having some major problems now."

"What's going on?" she asked.

"Well, long story short, two of the girls are dating the same guy. They didn't know it at first, but when they found out, they set up this tight plan to bust him, which we did. But then Alexis got back together with him anyway."

"Oooooh, it sounds like you guys have some *Young and the Restless* drama going on." Rosita laughed.

"You don't even know the half of it." I pushed something else out of Angelica's reach before continuing. "Now, Camille, she's the other one, is trying to get even with Alexis. And I just have a bad feeling somebody's gonna really get hurt."

"Wow," Rosita said.

"I've been thinking maybe I should go say something to Alexis, I don't know, maybe warn her."

"You know that's gonna make Camille mad?"

I nodded.

"But let me ask you this. If it was you, would you want to know what Camille was planning?" Rosita asked matter-of-factly.

I thought about it a minute. "Without a doubt."

"Then that's your answer on how you should handle this." Rosita stood up. "Ask yourself how sorry you'd be if something happens to Alexis and you could've done something to prevent it." Rosita leaned over and kissed Angelica before heading back to the bedroom. "I'm going to lie back down." She stopped at the edge of the hallway, turned around, and looked at me. "Angel, I know this has you bummed, but this really is nothing. If you want to know what major problems are, come live in my world for a little while." She didn't smile as she walked away.

To me, my problems were still major and if I didn't do anything else, I had to find a way to deal with them.

17

Angel

I was torn as I stood outside the huge front doors at Alexis's house. If I went inside, Camille might never forgive me. If I didn't and Keysha and her girls really hurt Alexis, I'd never forgive myself.

I wasn't exactly sure what I should do. I did know one thing: This had gone on for way too long. Camille was going to try and get the letter to Keysha today and I needed to somehow warn Alexis. The last thing I wanted was for her to get jumped somewhere out by herself. I'd thought about it all day and Rosita was right—I would be sick if something happened and I didn't do anything to prevent it.

I took a deep breath and rang the doorbell. Sonja answered the door so quickly, she had to have been standing on the other side.

"Hello, Miss Angel," she said.

"Hi, how are you?" I asked. "Is Alexis in?"

"Yes, please come in," Sonja said, stepping aside.

I walked through the spacious foyer and into the kitchen. The size of their kitchen was unbelievable. It was huge. There was a stove in the middle of the room and a refrigerator built into the wall. There was even a television built into the refrigerator. Alexis's mother was sitting at the breakfast bar reading *Vogue*. She had on a pink satin lounging robe and actually looked like she could've been in one of the magazine's ads or something.

"Well, hello, Angel," she said as I walked into the room. "It's been much too long. And I can't tell you how glad I am to see you." She closed the magazine. "Would you please tell me what is going on with my daughter? It's obvious something is wrong. She's been walking around here for the last two days acting like her best friend just died. I told her all of that frowning and unhappiness is going to give her wrinkles. Of course when I try to find out what's wrong, she claims it's nothing. But I'm her mother, I know better."

I forced a smile. I know how much Alexis hated having her mom all up in her business, but I could also tell she wasn't going to let me go upstairs until I told her something.

"We just kinda had a little fight in the Good Girlz. It

has everybody bummed out. I came by today to see if we can work it all out."

Her mother looked relieved as she pointed upstairs. "Well, please, by all means. She's upstairs in her room. She doesn't even have her television or her radio on. She's just lying across the bed, sulking."

I flashed another smile, then turned and headed up the winding staircase. I was confused. Why was Alexis so upset when she was the reason for the fight in the first place?

I knocked on her bedroom door and it swung open. I poked my head inside, immediately taking in the queen-size canopy bed, sofa, entertainment center, desk, dresser, and vanity table. The room looked like a princess lived in it. It was enough to bring anyone out of a depression. Anyone but Alexis, I guess. "Hey, Alexis."

She turned and looked at me, then laid her head back down on her pillow. "What do you want? I thought you guys weren't talking to me."

"Look," I said as I walked into her room. "Yes, we were mad, because what you did was foul. But you're still our girl, so we need to try to work this out."

"Seems to me like you guys already worked it out," she snapped.

"Can I just talk to you without the attitude just for a minute?"

"Whatever," she said. I couldn't believe she had the nerve to be acting mad. She was the one at fault.

"I just came by today because I wanted to talk to you."

I was hoping maybe if she could help me understand her reasons for getting back with Anthony, I could explain it to Camille and Jasmine and we could all go back to being friends.

"Talk," she said, still not looking at me.

"I don't understand how you can get back with Anthony. Especially after what he did to you guys. But at the same time, I don't want us to lose our friendship behind this. Camille is very hurt. So hurt that . . . " I said as I toyed with my belt.

Alexis finally turned over and looked at me. "So hurt that what? Finish what you were about to say."

I was trying to decide if I was going to continue. Oh well, I'd come this far, I might as well finish.

"So hurt that all she can think about is revenge."

Alexis raised her eyebrows. "What kind of revenge?"

"She plans to tell Anthony's ex about you." Camille was going to be so mad but I had to warn Alexis. I wouldn't go into all the details, but she needed to know. "She's hoping Keysha will find you somewhere and jump you."

"Are you talking about that crazy girl who jumped you guys?"

I nodded. Alexis looked dumbfounded as her eyes began to water. "So Camille is trying to get me beat up?" she finally said.

I nodded again.

"That's messed up."

"Alexis," I pointed out, my voice soft, "what you did was pretty messed up, too."

Alexis just stared at me as the tears began to trickle down her cheeks. "You don't understand."

"Well, help me understand. I think Camille is going too far, but none of us can see how you could do this."

Alexis started crying now as she buried her face in her hands. "I had planned to sleep with him, Angel," she sobbed.

My eyes grew wide. Since the day we met, Alexis had prided herself on being a virgin. She'd even gone to one of those chastity conferences when she was fourteen and pledged to save herself for her husband. She had a chastity ring and everything.

"You've got to be kidding me. When? Why didn't you say anything?" I sat down next to her.

"I was going to tell you all the night we found out about Anthony. I just thought that he was the one, so I let him convince me to do it. He told me he loved me and he said if I didn't do it, I couldn't blame him if he messed around on me." She sniffed as she wiped her tears. "I even gave him my chastity ring. I can't believe I was so stupid. I've had guys shoot me all kinds of lines before but I never fell for them. Why did I do it this time?"

I didn't know what to say. I was in shock, especially because she had been so adamant about waiting.

"But you didn't sleep with him, did you? You said you were *going to*. You didn't actually do it . . . right?"

"No, but only because I found out about him playing me and Camille. I was about to go against everything I believed in. I was about to give him the most special thing I own," she cried.

I wanted to ask her how she could even think about doing that, but I'd done my share of stupid things. I mean, who was I to judge? I'd gotten pregnant on my first time with a boy I now can't stand.

"Angel, me deciding to sleep with him—that's deep for me, the fact that I was about to do it, period. That's just not something I can take lightly." She sniffled. "He made a complete fool out of me."

I took her hand. "Which is even more reason why I don't understand why you got back with him."

She sighed and wiped her face. "My father always says that you should keep your friends close and your enemies closer. That's what I was doing. That little payback at the beach wasn't enough for me. I'm going to make Anthony pay for what he did and the only way I could do that was to make him think I forgave him and was so wrapped up in him that I wanted him back."

I looked at her and shook my head. "So this is all fake?"

She nodded.

"Why didn't you tell us?"

"When I tried to, Camille started going off, talking about I'm fake and stuff. I just said forget it. I'd handle Anthony myself."

I squeezed Alexis's hand. "Girl, I am so sorry. You should've made us listen."

Alexis sniffled again. "I'm used to it in my life. Nobody ever listens to me. Nobody cares about my feelings. So

I did what I always do—I decided to deal with it on my own."

I knew her parents were always so busy—her dad with his business and her mom with all her social engagements. Any free time her mom did have (which wasn't much) was spent visiting Alexis's sister, Sharon, who was autistic and lived in a special school, or moping about the fact that Sharon was in that school at all.

"You know what," I said, trying to lighten the mood. "We are going to call Camille right now and tell her and Jasmine to meet us at the mall so we can talk. They need to know what you just told me."

I got up and walked over to her phone before she could protest. Honestly, she didn't even look like she wanted to. She just seemed relieved that someone was making a move toward patching up our friendship.

18

Jasmine

This had definitely better be good. Angel had called me at home and told me to get Camille to come meet her and Alexis at Memorial City Mall in the food court.

Of course I had to ask her what was going on. She would only say that we all just really needed to talk and hear Alexis out. I didn't know if I wanted to hear what Alexis had to say, but Camille was getting out of control so we had to do something.

It had been hard trying to convince Camille to go to the mall. She'd lost that happy-go-lucky attitude and was now back to being in a funk. Luckily, she needed to get a new cell phone earpiece, so she finally decided to give in and go.

We had gotten Camille's new Bluetooth and were now

sitting in the food court, sipping on some Chick-fil-A shakes. We were laughing when the smile suddenly left Camille's face. I turned to see what she was looking at. Alexis and Angel were walking up.

"I should have known you guys were up to something," she said, standing.

"Would you wait a minute?" I said, grabbing her arm.

Camille snatched her arm away. "No. I don't know what kind of game y'all trying to run, but I don't wanna hear it." She cut her eyes at Alexis. "I told you, I'm done with her."

"Camille," Angel said, trying to keep her voice reasonable. "You remember what you did when you were trying to get that talk show?"

Camille had gotten her then-boyfriend's dad to pull some strings and help her win a spot as the host of a teen talk show on Channel 2. She was up against Alexis and had basically stabbed her in the back to get the job.

Camille cut her eyes at Angel. I know she hated that Angel went there and reminded her of all the dirty tricks she pulled. "And your point would be?" she snapped, rolling her eyes.

"Well, we gave you another chance," Angel continued.

"Yeah," I chimed in. "So that means you need to give her one as well because you were completely out of order with that whole thing."

"Just hear me out," Alexis said softly.

"Fine," Camille huffed as she spun toward Alexis. "I'll hear you out because I would love to hear what possible reason you could have for stabbing me in the back."

"I'm not really back together with Anthony," she said, diverting her gaze.

"What does that mean?" Camille said. "Angel saw you with him. And you dang sure didn't deny it. In fact, you admitted you got back together with him so don't be trying to lie your way out of it now."

"I am back with him, but I'm not."

"That doesn't make any sense," Camille said, twisting up her lip. "Either you are or you aren't."

Alexis hesitated and took a deep breath. I was waiting, too.

"I . . . I planned to lose my virginity to Anthony."

"What!" Camille exclaimed. "You slept with him?"

"No, but I was going to," Alexis said, tears forming in her eyes. "On the day we found out about him seeing us both."

Camille sat back down, stunned. "Umphh, he was pressuring me, too, but I stood my ground."

"Wow," I added, just as shocked as Camille. "You were so serious about saving yourself. He must've really run some game on you. Besides, I thought you had taken some kind of pledge or something."

"I did. That's why I couldn't just let this go," Alexis said as she and Angel sat down, too.

"But nothing happened, so it's okay," Angel interjected. It was obvious she was trying to make Alexis feel better.

"I know," Alexis replied. "The fact that I didn't actually do it is the only reason I'm not completely losing it. But knowing that I just let Anthony convince me to give up something that meant so much . . . I just can't let it go . . ." She let her voice trail off as a tear trickled down her face.

Camille must have finally seen how much Alexis was hurting, because her tone softened.

"Dang, Alexis. I didn't know."

"Nobody did. I mean, I planned to tell you all that night, but I never got the chance." She took a deep breath. "I was really, really mad when I found out about you. Yeah, we busted him and everything, but to me, it wasn't enough, especially when I heard him and his friends laughing about it when I went up to his school to try and ask him how he could do this to me. He was showing off in front of his boys, acting like it was no big deal. He tried to turn the whole beach scene around like he was some stud that had two girls fighting over him. It just ticked me off. I wanted him to pay for real. I had to find a way to make him pay."

"But the whole beach party thing. I thought we were through with him after that," Camille said.

"I wanted it to be over but watching him act out, I don't know. It just wasn't enough," Alexis responded.

"So you got with him as payback?" I said. "This isn't making any sense."

"Basically," Alexis replied. "I hadn't even figured out how I was gon' get him back yet. I just knew that I needed to keep him close to me until I came up with a plan."

"Wow," I said.

Camille still looked like she didn't know whether to believe Alexis or not. "So why didn't you tell us this from the jump?"

Alexis just stared at her. "Did you give me a chance?"

Camille bit down on her lip.

Alexis continued before she could answer. "No, you didn't. You just started going off, calling me all kinds of names. I was trying to explain to you then what I was doing, but you didn't want to hear it."

A remorseful look crossed Camille's face. "Well, you still should've said something."

Alexis shrugged. "Maybe I should have. But I felt like you said what you really meant."

Camille shifted her gaze to the floor. "You know I was just mad. I didn't mean most of that stuff," she muttered.

"Whatever," Alexis said. "Just forget it. I know you were mad. I would've been, too. But you gotta understand, I can't let him get away with this."

"Well, I'm with you if you wanna know the truth," I interjected. I'd been trying to let them have their little moment, but I needed to put my two cents in. "So what's up?"

"Well," Alexis said, "I was thinking on the way over here that maybe we can use the whole idea you had about getting me back."

Camille's eyes grew wide as she looked at Angel. "I can't believe you told her."

Angel shrugged. "I had to."

"Don't worry about it," Alexis said. "I actually don't think that it's such a bad idea. Only we need to direct Keysha's anger straight at Anthony. Let's let Keysha and her ghetto cousin deal with him."

Camille thought about it a minute, then nodded. "Okay, okay, I'm feeling that."

"No doubt," I added.

"I'm in with whatever you guys want to do," Angel said.

Alexis finally smiled. "We're about to show Anthony Vickers that he messed with the wrong friends this time 'cause he's about to pay for his play."

I couldn't agree more.

19

Jasmine

Operation Make Anthony Pay was in full effect. Camille and Alexis had actually banded together with a passion I'd never seen before.

They'd agreed that Alexis would continue seeing Anthony and acting like everything was cool. Camille had done some digging and found a bunch of information on Keysha. Camille was going to make a really good reporter one day because she was all on the Internet and had found out stuff I didn't even know she could find out.

"All right, it's going down today," Camille said.

It was hard to believe that it had been only a week since we'd hatched our little plan. I'd even gotten in the game a little bit, by using Donovan like he'd used me. I made him think that we were no longer friends with Alexis since she had chosen to stay with Anthony.

We'd dropped the letter off at Keysha's about an hour ago, after waiting outside her house for her to come home from school. We were banking on her going straight over to Anthony's after receiving his gift and note asking her to be there by four. As luck would have it, Shoshanna pulled up, with Keysha in the passenger seat.

"That's what I'm talkin' about," Camille whispered as she peered over the steering wheel. We watched as they walked up to the front door and picked up the note and package. "This is working out perfectly. Shoshanna ain't gonna do nothing but pump her up." Camille beamed.

That must've been exactly what happened, because the next thing we knew they turned around and headed back to Shoshanna's car. Judging by the big, stupid grin on Keysha's face, they couldn't have been heading anywhere but to Anthony's.

Luckily, we beat them by about five minutes so we were already parked by the time they got to Anthony's house. "There they are," Camille said, pointing to the beat-up Chevy Impala Shoshanna was driving. "That girl looks like a straight gangsta chick." As planned, Camille quickly sent Alexis a text message to her iPhone.

I felt a twinge of nervousness. Shoshanna had her hair braided straight back. She looked like Queen Latifah did in *Set It Off*. I relaxed when I saw the police car parked down the street. We'd had no idea how Keysha was going to act, or if she'd have anyone with her, so Camille had her cousin, who was a cop, hang nearby just in case. She told him that Alexis was having some trouble with her boyfriend's ex and she wanted to avoid a fight.

On cue, Alexis walked out of Anthony's house. He had his arm draped around her and was kissing all over her. She had on a black Baby Phat outfit with a matching purse. It was the exact same one we'd sent to Keysha. I definitely wasn't feeling spending money on an outfit for Keysha, but Alexis was gung ho and since it wasn't my money, I let it go.

We'd put a card in the box and signed it, "Please take me back. I'll wait at my house for you until four. Love, Vic."

Personally, I thought the plan was shaky at first, because I wasn't sure Keysha would actually go see Anthony, and I definitely didn't know if Alexis could convince Anthony to come pick her up and take her back to his place. But she had no doubt she could persuade him to take her to his house since his mom didn't get home till really late. And she was right because everything seemed to be coming together perfectly.

"Look!" Camille said, getting excited. "I think they see them."

I leaned in and watched as the Impala turned into Anthony's driveway. The passenger door flew open before the car came to a complete stop. Keysha jumped out and stomped up the sidewalk. I could see the fear all over Alexis's face. Anthony looked shocked himself. I'm sure he knew how psycho Keysha was, so he had to know things were definitely about to jump off.

"Oh, it's about to be on!" Keysha screamed.

Camille motioned for her cousin and he pulled out and slowly drove in front of Anthony's house.

Shoshanna had just gotten out of the car herself, looking like she was about to beat Alexis down, when she noticed the police car.

"Keysha, chill!" She motioned toward the cop car. "You know I'm on probation."

Keysha slowed her pace as the car passed. You could tell she was still about to go off.

Alexis knew that was her cue. She took off running toward us and jumped into the front seat.

"Let's go. I don't even want to be around because she's about to kill him," she said, out of breath.

We all cracked up laughing as Camille pulled the car out. "Girl, you looked like you were running a marathon the way you took off."

"I don't care. I just didn't want to be around when she lost it." Camille was just about to turn the corner when Alexis added, "Wait. On second thought, just circle the block. I want to see this. I want to witness him get beat down by Keysha and Shoshanna."

"Is your cousin going to stick around?" Angel asked nervously.

"Naw, he's in the middle of his shift. So I was lucky to get him to come by at all. He was just making sure that nothing happened to Alexis. But I would like to see how that dog weasels his way out of this, too," Camille added.

We circled the block and came back in just enough time to see Keysha push Anthony's chest. Shoshanna had a finger pointed in Anthony's face. He looked a little scared, but you could tell he was getting mad himself.

"Knock him upside his head," Alexis snarled through gritted teeth. "Tear his guts out."

We all turned toward her.

"Okay, sorry, I'm getting a little carried away but I hope she slaps the mess out of him. Or better yet, let Shoshanna's gangsta behind pull some of her hood moves on him."

We laughed. "Wait a minute, where's he going?" I said as I noticed Anthony quickly heading toward his truck.

Both Keysha and Shoshanna followed him. They were yelling at him the entire way.

"Dang, I wish I could hear what they were saying," Camille said.

"I bet she's giving him a piece of her mind." Alexis laughed. "That's what he gets."

Anthony unlocked the door and climbed into the truck. Keysha was banging on the hood, still screaming as he drove over the grass to get around Shoshanna's car.

Alexis laughed. "Coward!"

We watched as Anthony sped off down the street. Shoshanna and Keysha didn't waste any time. They ran and jumped in their car and took off after him.

"Come on, come on," Alexis said. "Let's follow them."

"Guys," Angel said, "don't you think we've done enough?"

"Unh-unh. I need to see how this all plays out." Alexis giggled.

"I'm with you, girl," Camille threw in. "I want to see them catch him and beat him down." She put the car in drive and followed them.

Anthony was flying in his yellow Dakota pickup truck. Keysha was driving the Impala as they sped out of the neighborhood and down Martin Luther King Drive.

"Look how fast that fool is driving!" Camille exclaimed.

"And Keysha is hanging in there with him," I said, eyeing Camille's speedometer, "We're doing sixty, so they have to be going at least seventy-five."

"Oh, my God," Angel said. "I can't believe she's chasing him."

Anthony had gotten to a stoplight when Keysha rammed her car into the back of him.

"Did you see that?" Alexis gasped. We were several cars behind them, but we could still see everything clear as day. "That fool just hit him! I told you guys she was crazy!"

Anthony swerved the truck into another lane and took off, running the red light and narrowly missing an oncoming car.

"Don't lose 'em. Don't lose 'em!" Alexis shouted as our light turned green. We sped around the car in front of us and caught up with Keysha just as she followed Anthony onto the 610 freeway.

"I can not believe y'all got us up here in a freaking high-speed chase," I barked as I looked at the speedometer again. We were now up to seventy-five miles an hour. I was down with this whole plan at first, but this was taking things a bit too far.

"Be careful, Camille," Angel said as we darted between two cars.

Camille ignored us both as she navigated her car in and out of a bunch of different lanes, struggling to keep up with Keysha and Anthony. Both her and Alexis looked like madwomen as they excitedly watched the chase unfold. I was amazed a cop hadn't stopped any of us yet, we were all going so fast.

Anthony had just taken the overpass off one freeway heading onto another. The way he was flying, I just knew it was a matter of time before we had a trail of cops behind us.

"Slow down before you get a ticket!" I yelled.

"Girl, I'm not about to lose them," Camille shot back.

"He'd better slow down!" Angel said as we watched Anthony's truck tilt on two wheels as it went around the bend.

Keysha hit the same turn; but this time, when her car tilted to the side, the wheels didn't come back down. We watched in horror as the Impala hit the guardrail and flipped over.

"Oh, my God!" someone, I don't even know who, screamed.

The car flipped over again, then bounced onto the feeder road below.

"Ohmigod, ohmigod, ohmigod!" Camille said, slowing down.

All of us were scared beyond belief, mouths open in shock. I don't know if Anthony didn't see what happened or didn't care, because he kept going.

"What are we gonna do?" Camille said, starting to panic. By this time we were rounding the bend ourselves. Traffic had come to a crawl because of the accident. I leaned over to the window and looked out. The car was upside down and smoke was coming from the hood.

"It looks like people are stopping!" I said. "Somebody's trying to pull them out."

"Go down there," Angel said. "Get off at the next exit and go down there!"

"Are you crazy?" I snapped. "We can't go down there. We're the reason she was chasing him." I leaned back against the seat. "Oh no, they're going to blame us. This is all our fault." Visions of jail started to cloud my mind. In my neighborhood, jail was a common stop but I had always vowed that would never be my destiny. So the mere thought of doing time sent me into a panic.

"Ohhhh, I knew this wasn't a good idea," Angel said as tears started to form in her eyes. "What are we gonna do?"

"Just go, just go," I snapped. Camille did what several other cars had started doing, going across the grassy median to exit the freeway. She was shaking as she navigated the car away from the accident. Alexis was no good. She just sat in the passenger seat in a state of shock.

After about five minutes of driving, Camille said, "Where am I going?"

"Just pull over," I said, feeling like I had to take control of the situation.

Camille pulled off the freeway and into a Chevron gas station. She cut off the car and we sat in silence for a few minutes.

Finally, Alexis spoke. "I do not believe what just happened."

"Do you think they're dead?" Angel quietly asked.

"Man, I hope not," I said, trying to shake off the possibility.

"If they are, we are in so much trouble," Alexis whispered.

I banged my head against the headrest. "I can't go to jail, I can't go to jail."

"Why would we go to jail?" Angel asked.

"Don't you get it?" I yelled. "Keysha never would have been chasing him and this accident never would've happened if it wasn't for Alexis's stupid idea."

"My stupid idea?" Alexis spun around in her seat. "You were the one who was pushing for us to do *something* to get revenge in the first place! And I didn't see you complaining when Camille came up with the idea."

"Oh, so now it's my fault?" Camille interjected.

"Okay, guys, we really shouldn't be arguing like this," Angel said, trying to be the voice of reason.

We all just grew silent. Nobody knew what to do next. All I knew was that if Keysha and her cousin were seriously hurt, we were in some real trouble.

20

Angel

I'd hardly been able to concentrate all day long. Luckily, my mom was off, so she would be keeping Angelica. Ever since the accident yesterday, I hadn't even been able to think straight.

We'd finally made it home an hour and a half later with no idea what we were going to do. We did decide that we would never tell anyone we were the ones behind the accident. I don't know if that was the right choice but I was with Jasmine: I couldn't go to jail.

I'd prayed all night long that both Keysha and Shoshanna would be fine.

"Did you hear anything?" Jasmine said as she walked up to me after fifth period. We'd watched the news and they did have a story about the accident, but all they said was two girls were in critical condition at a local hospital. Another news story used the word "serious." I didn't know what that meant. Were they hurt a little bit? A lot? "Serious" had to be better than "critical," right?

"I haven't heard anything," I finally responded.

"Me either," said Camille, walking up and joining us as we headed to our Spanish class. "And I have been going crazy. I even broke down and tried to call Vic but he's not answering his phone."

"Oh, man. I can't believe we got caught up in the middle of this." I moaned.

"Who are you telling?" Camille said. "I should have just let it go."

"It's like Miss Rachel said—who are we to be trying to seek revenge?" I asked, shaking my head. " 'Vengeance is mine,' sayeth the Lord."

"Angel, I know you're right, but I'm not in the mood to hear a sermon, okay?" Jasmine said. "I'm already freakin' out as it is."

"Okay, fine," I responded. "But let me ask you this. If either one of them dies, can we really go to jail?"

"I don't know," Camille said. "Why does everyone keep asking me all the questions?"

"Look, don't be biting our heads off," Jasmine snapped.

Camille grunted. I could tell everybody was just stressing out.

"Maybe after school we can go ride by the hospital," I offered.

"What hospital?" Jasmine asked. "We don't even know where they took them."

"I guess you're right." I sighed.

"Dang, what are we gonna do?" Alexis asked.

"Can't you call your cousin the cop?" I suggested.

"Are you crazy?" Camille said. "If he puts two and two together, he's definitely going to tell my mom and she's going to make me turn myself in. Nope, not gonna happen."

"Then what are we gonna do?" I said.

"I have no idea." Camille sighed.

"Hey, y'all. What's up?" Tameka caught up with us outside the Spanish class. Camille took calculus right next door.

We all just stared at Tameka, but didn't respond. I knew nobody wanted to tell her what was going on because we didn't want to chance her telling Miss Rachel.

"Nothing," Jasmine finally replied.

Tameka looked at us skeptically. "Don't say nothing because I can tell from the look on your faces that something is going on."

Jasmine forced a smile. "Naw, it's nothing for real. Camille is stressing everybody out talking about her breakup with Anthony."

Tameka had learned bits and pieces about the whole situation when we talked about it at the Good Girlz meeting, but, of course, she didn't know everything. Tameka leaned in. "Speaking of Anthony, have I got some news for you." She smiled devilishly. "Y'all know I transferred from Kashmere, where both Anthony and his little skeezer girlfriend went."

"And?" Jasmine asked.

"And, so I got a call last night that Anthony's ex-girlfriend, Keysha, was in a bad car accident. Isn't Keysha the one who jumped you?" she asked, looking at Camille, who nodded. "Well, now you can say she got hers."

We were all dumbfounded at the pleasure Tameka seemed to take in talking about the accident.

"They don't know if she's going to make it," she continued.

"What do you mean, they don't know if she's going to make it?" I asked.

"Just what I said. Anyway, just thought y'all'd like to know. I need to get inside and finish my Spanish homework before she takes up our papers." Tameka went into the room. We all stood in shock.

"Oh, my God, what are we going to do?" Alexis said.

"We're not going to do anything," Jasmine replied.

"Yeah, we were nowhere near the accident when it happened," Camille said, trying to sound convincing.

"But we were," I protested.

"Look, we weren't there. That's our story and we need to stick to it," Jasmine said.

"But what if Anthony tells them we were the ones that started all this?" I know I was trippin' but I was really starting to freak out. I couldn't do jail.

"He's not going to do that," Camille said. "Because he'd

be in just as much trouble as us. Besides, even if he did, it would be his word against ours."

"What if one of those red light cameras they have all over town caught us on tape?" I know I was reaching, but panic was really starting to set in.

Camille huffed. "There are no cameras. Anthony isn't going to come forward. We're straight. As long as we all stay on the same page. Understand?" I didn't understand, but I had a little girl to think about. So I really didn't know what choice I had but to keep my mouth shut.

21

Jasmine

"So Tameka, have you heard anything else about Keysha?" I asked, trying my best to sound like I was making casual conversation while we waited on the Good Girlz meeting to start.

It had been three days since the accident and although we'd tried not to talk about it, we were all nervous wrecks. Now the key was to make it through this meeting without somebody feeling the need to confess. Miss Rachel had a way of making us feel guilty and I was really worried that someone would feel the need to come clean with her. I cut my eyes over at Angel. Somehow I just knew she was going to be that somebody. Angel was sitting there, nervously chewing her fingernails. She wouldn't make eye contact with me. Yep, she would definitely be the one to snap.

After Tameka told us about Keysha, we called Alexis and filled her in on what was said. She agreed that we should keep our mouths shut. All of us thought it was for the best, but I could tell it was a decision we weren't all comfortable with.

"Oh, yeah," Tameka said, happy to bring us gossip. "She's still in the hospital. She's gonna be there for a while. I heard both of her legs are broken. They don't know if she'll ever walk again. And that's if she even pulls through this. They are supposedly really concerned because her heart rate keeps dropping."

"Oh, no," Angel moaned.

"Her cousin was with her. They said she's gonna be fine. I think she even went home yesterday. But Keysha, well, I heard it's pretty bad," Tameka said.

"Oh, no," Angel repeated, biting the nails on her other hand.

Tameka narrowed her eyes. "What? Why are you freaking out? I'd've thought you'd be happy. This is Keysha's payback for jumping you guys."

"Well, if that isn't the most absurd thing I've ever heard." We all looked up to see Rachel standing in the door. "I told you before, God doesn't work like that." She walked in and stood at the front of the room, shaking her head at us. "You girls should know better than to think God would purposely hurt somebody as a way of getting back at them." She then began to give us a lecture about the fact that while God was vengeful, He didn't bring harm to people in the form of revenge.

I didn't know if Keysha's accident was some sort of payback from God or what. All I knew was that Keysha wouldn't be in the hospital if it wasn't for us. If she didn't pull through, I was really going to have a hard time dealing with it. Shoot, if that was her payback, what would be ours?

I could tell Camille felt the same way, especially because this whole thing about getting Keysha involved was her idea. She was sitting a few chairs down, with a faraway look in her eyes.

Rachel opened her Bible. "I had been looking for something to inspire you girls, and I found it in Leviticus. It says, 'Do not seek revenge or bear a grudge against one of your people, but love your neighbor as yourself.'"

I knew it was her job to put this all in a religious context, but right about now, that wasn't helping me a whole lot.

"Miss Rachel," I said, raising my hand, finally deciding to say what had been on my mind. "How can you say that? I mean, I'm not trying to be disrespectful, but you said yourself you used to do a lot of hateful things trying to get revenge on your boyfriend's girlfriend when you were a teenager."

Rachel nodded like she was recalling something. "I did a whole lot of things I'm not proud of, which is why I feel like I can talk to you now. I've been where you are. I know what it's like to want to get revenge on someone. But I've also grown a lot over the years and learned some lessons the hard way. Truth be told, I'm battling with some demons now. But trust me, payback never pays off. Now, don't get me wrong—my walk is still difficult sometimes. I'm far from perfect, but I just want to get you guys to see that there's nothing to be gained by trying to go tit for tat with someone."

We all sat in silence.

"So we're wrong for wanting revenge?" Camille finally asked.

"No, on the contrary," Rachel answered. "The desire for revenge is a normal, natural emotion that we all feel from time to time. But what should we do in situations like that?"

I couldn't wait to hear the answer to that because what we'd done was definitely not it.

"I'll tell you what you do," Rachel continued. "When things get tough, when people make you so mad that you just want to harm them, you trust God. You don't take matters into your own hands. As a person who has done both, I can tell you, trusting God is much better."

She smiled at us. I guess she could tell that her words were sinking in. I glanced at Angel. She had her eyes lowered. I'd been worried about her. Now, I was the one feeling the need to confess.

"Vengeance belongs to God," Rachel continued. "If you act out of a sense of outrage, you probably won't think things through before you act. Because I guarantee if you think out all the things that could happen because of what you plan to do, you will have a change of heart. That's why you need to turn those emotions over to God and let Him handle the revenge."

I was confused. Did Rachel know we were behind the accident, or was she just speaking generally? No, if she knew, she definitely would be going off on us.

"But doesn't the Bible also say something about an eye for an eye?" Camille said, her voice still shaky.

"It does, but I think we've taken that out of context over the years. The Bible is clear that you don't do evil just because someone did evil to you. If they did the wrong thing, you do the right thing. Don't get involved in the business of trying to get even—making sure everybody gets what they deserve. That's God's job and He's really good at it. Instead, we're supposed to try to get along as much as possible. God will take care of justice. It may not be when we want it. It may not be how we want it. But He will make sure that justice is done."

"And it was," Tameka said with authority.

Rachel shook her head. "That's not your call to make."

I didn't care whose call it was. The bottom line remained—we were the reason Keysha was in the hospital, and if what Miss Rachel was saying was true, it would be just a matter of time before God extracted some justice on us as well.

22

Jasmine

Okay, I know I'm not crazy. I turned around again and looked at the black Buick that seemed to be following us. It had dark, tinted windows, so I couldn't make out the driver, just that there were at least two people in the car. "Alexis, do you see that black car back there? They've been following us since we left the church."

Alexis looked up at her rearview mirror. Angel and Camille turned around as well.

"You're just being paranoid," Camille said, turning back around in the backseat.

"I am not crazy." Where I come from, you notice things like strange cars following you, so I'd spotted the car immediately. "You stopped and got gas. And if the car wasn't following us, it would've been long gone. But it's still behind us."

"Maybe it's a different car," Alexis replied.

I sat back. I wasn't convinced. Something wasn't right.

"Pull off like you're getting off the freeway and see what happens," I said.

Alexis huffed like I was bothering her or something but she did pull off. And a few seconds later, so did the black Buick.

"See, I told y'all!" I said, sitting up in the seat. The driver made sure there were at least two cars between us, but they were definitely following us.

"Dang," Alexis said as a worried look finally crept up on her face.

"Pull into that Burger King on the corner," Angel said, looking nervous herself.

Alexis navigated her car into the parking lot. We sat there for a minute trying to figure out what to do. The Buick didn't turn into the parking lot but instead passed right by the restaurant.

Alexis relaxed her shoulders. "See, we're getting all worked up for nothing."

"Yeah, Jas. You got us all freakin' out. Let's go," Camille said.

Alexis put the car in reverse and was about to back out when the black Buick quickly pulled up behind us, blocking us in our parking space.

My heart started racing. I told them I wasn't imagining things!

"Oh, my God," Camille said as she watched the passenger side door of the Buick open. I saw the blond braids first, then Shoshanna came limping toward our car, the cast on her leg obviously slowing her down. Three other people got out of the Buick as well. All of them looked just as rough as she did.

"Umph, well if it isn't the chicks that tried to kill me," Shoshanna said as she and one of the girls went to Alexis's side of the car and the other two came around to my side. Shoshanna used her fists to pound on the car. "Open the window. Don't punk out now! You all big and bad!"

Now, I admit I can be tough, but right about now I felt like peeing in my pants.

Angel looked like she was about to have an asthma attack and Camille looked like she was having flashbacks of her last beat-down. "Call the cops," Angel whispered, motioning toward Alexis's cell phone.

"It's cool," Alexis shot back. "She's probably all talk."

I wanted to ask her who was kidding? Alexis cracked the window. "What do you want?" she said.

"Get out the car and see," Shoshanna snapped, cracking her knuckles. She looked pretty good for someone who had been in a near fatal accident. With the exception of the cast and a bunch of scars on her face, which I wasn't sure she didn't have before the accident, you would have never known she had nearly been killed a couple of weeks ago.

"Alexis, you'd better not unlock that door. Do not get out the car," I hissed. I could fight, but no way could I take these four gangsta girls. We were as good as dead if we got out.

"Get out the car before I bust this window!" Shoshanna barked.

"What should I do?" Alexis mumbled.

"Back up. Hit their car. Run over the sidewalk, anything. We need to get away from here," I said, grabbing Alexis's cell phone. *So much for being all talk,* I thought as I tried to punch in 9-1-1. "These girls are probably packin'." I looked down at the cell phone and watched as it beeped and went dead. "Oh, no, your phone is dead! Camille, where's your phone?"

Camille sat frozen, staring out the window in terror. "Come on!" Shoshanna banged on the window again, causing all of us to jump. "Don't act like you scared now! You wanna try to set somebody up, dang near get me killed. Got my cousin laid all up in the hospital. Come on out here and show us how bad you really are."

I wished I could be anywhere but here at this very moment. I couldn't help but think that maybe this was our payback. "Where's your phone?" I shouted at Camille again.

She snapped out of her daze. "I . . . I left it at home."

I blew a frustrated breath. "Alexis, you don't have a car charger?" She shook her head. "Good grief, why do y'all even have cell phones?" I snapped, trying to figure out what we were going to do.

"Quita!" Shoshanna said, motioning toward one of the

girls on my side. "Get the baseball bat out the trunk. We're about to get crunk up in here!"

"Are we just gonna sit here and let them kill us?" I frantically asked.

"You're the one always ready for a fight," Camille said as Quita ran back to their car. "What should we do?"

"Ummm, we should get outta here. And fast," I responded. "Run them over, hit the car, just do something."

Alexis looked like she was contemplating what to do. God must've heard our cries because Quita had just popped the trunk when two police officers came out of Burger King, rubbing their stomachs like they'd just had a big meal.

They looked at Shoshanna and the girls surrounding our car. For a minute, I felt a sense of relief, especially when I saw them headed our way. Shoshanna and her friends stood up and tried to look innocent. But when the officers kept walking past our car, I knew I was about to lose our only chance at getting out of this without getting hurt.

I quickly put down my window. "Excuse me. Excuse me, Mr. Officer," I called out.

Both policemen turned back toward me.

"We really need some help over here," I said nervously.

Shoshanna shot me a look like she wanted to strangle me right then and there. The officers walked back over to our car. The two girls on my side stepped back as the officers approached my window.

"Yes, little lady. What can I do for you?" the taller officer said.

I really didn't want to be a snitch, but I really didn't want to die either. I glanced back at Shoshanna's mean mug and knew that if I didn't say something it was all over. "Yes sir," I began. "We're being harassed by these four girls and we'd really like to get some assistance in getting them to leave us alone so we can leave peacefully."

The officers looked at the girls. Shoshanna bit down on her bottom lip, her eyes narrowing in anger.

"Is this correct?" the first officer asked.

"We ain't harassing nobody," Quita said.

"Yeah, we were just here trying to talk," Shoshanna added, trying her best to look innocent.

"Officer, we really would like to leave," Alexis leaned over and said. "But as you can see, they've blocked us in. They followed us here, threatening us. Now they won't let us out."

"Let me see some ID," the second officer said, walking over to Shoshanna.

"I ain't got no ID," she snapped.

"Who's driving this car then?" he asked, pointing to the Buick. "I know somebody better have a license."

"It's my car," Quita said.

Shoshanna balled up her fists. "You need to be talking to them about that car wreck they caused a couple of weeks ago that almost killed me and left my cousin paralyzed."

The officer still standing by my door looked down at me. "What is she talking about?"

I froze. I didn't know what to say or do.

"Check your police files," Shoshanna shouted, getting worked up again. "Check 'em! The accident happened at 610 and 288 two weeks ago. They caused it, all 'cause they tryin' to stick it to some dude."

"Okay, miss, I'm going to need you to calm down," the officer near Shoshanna said.

Instead, she started shouting as she moved toward Alexis's window again. "Naw, I'ma calm down all right. I'ma calm down when I got my foot up her—"

"Miss!" the officer admonished as he stepped in between the car and Shoshanna. "I said calm down before I arrest you! I need you to step away from the car. Get back in your vehicle and leave before I take you to jail."

"Arrest them!" she shouted, pointing at us.

"This is your last warning," he said sternly.

"Come on, girl," one of her other friends said.

Shoshanna's nostrils flared as she gritted her teeth so hard, they seemed like they would crack. I swear if that officer hadn't been there, I really believe she would've killed us with her bare hands.

Her friend gently pulled her away. Shoshanna nodded as she backed up. "Watch your back. You feel me? Watch your back. All of you."

We all were shaking something crazy as we watched them get into the car and drive off. The other officer leaned down. "Now which of you young ladies is going to tell me what she's talking about?"

I silently stared at the officer. I dang sure wasn't about to tell on myself but I wasn't going to lie either. So I just kept my mouth closed.

"Oh, so you're not talking now?" he said.

The other officer motioned toward Alexis. "Miss, step out of the car, please."

Alexis looked at us, a scared expression on her face, before she turned back around and got out.

"Now what was that girl talking about?" he asked.

Alexis stared down at the ground. The officer seemed to be getting frustrated. "How about we just go on downtown and you can tell it to the judge?"

Alexis looked up, her eyes wide. "She thinks we're responsible for this accident that they were involved in."

"Were you?"

"N-not exactly," Alexis stuttered.

"Look, you can tell me now, or you can tell me later, after spending the night in jail for obstruction of justice."

Alexis turned and looked at us in the car again, her eyes pleading for us to tell her what to do. I wasn't about to tell her to lie. We were in enough trouble as it was.

"Miss, look at me," the officer said. Alexis turned back to him. "If you were involved in that accident in any shape, form, or fashion, you need to let me know now. We will investigate and if we find out you were involved, you could be in big trouble."

I took a deep breath. My head was pounding.

"Okay, okay. It was an accident. We didn't mean for her to take off after him." Alexis rushed the words out. "We just wanted to pay Anthony back for trying to date me and Camille, who really thought his name was Vic. We just wanted Keysha, his ex who is in the hospital, to get mad and maybe cuss him out or something. But Anthony took off and Keysha followed him and they were going really, really fast and when they went around the curve, Keysha lost control of the car and crashed. But we didn't mean for any of it to happen." Alexis started crying.

"Okay, slow down," the officer said, trying to take in everything Alexis had said.

"I remember that accident," the other officer said.

"Are we going to jail?" Alexis sniffed.

"No, but you do need to call your parents because we all need to take a trip downtown," the first officer said. "You can follow us. And no tricky stuff. We have your license plate number."

Alexis wiped her eyes and nodded. She got back in the car, where we all sat in shock. She slowly pulled out, following the officer. "I can't believe I have to call my parents," she said.

I didn't respond. I know I didn't want to call my mother, and from the look on Jasmine's face, that wasn't an option for her either.

"I say we call Miss Rachel," Camille said.

"Yeah," Jasmine chimed in. "Miss Rachel. She's gonna

be mad, but right about now, she's our only hope at getting out of this mess."

"I agree," I added. *Dear God, just let me get out of this mess,* I prayed silently, *and You don't ever have to worry about trouble finding its way to my doorstep again.*

23

Angel

Thank God for Miss Rachel and her connections. Luckily, she had a relationship with one of the police officers in the juvenile division. A woman named Lydia Patterson. Alexis and Jasmine said she's the same lady who called Rachel when they got into trouble for shoplifting last year. She'd stepped up to the plate once again and now Rachel was on her way instead of our parents.

But knowing Rachel, we weren't out of the woods just yet. She was going to let us have it and I just knew she was going to end up telling our parents anyway.

We all sat nervously around the large oak conference room table. The officer who had brought us back here had made it clear that we were not under arrest. He said they just "wanted our assistance in investigating the accident." But I still didn't like being here because honestly, I was scared that it was just a matter of time before we were under arrest.

At Officer Patterson's request, they waited to question us until Rachel got there, so for now we were in the conference room by ourselves.

"Okay, so what are we gonna tell them?" Camille whispered.

"Man, we need to tell them the truth," I replied. "Because I'm already stressed out. I can't be remembering a whole bunch of different lies."

"What if they take us all in different rooms?" Alexis asked.

"Well, we should come up with something now, then we just stick to our stories," Camille said.

"Naw, y'all. I'm with Angel," Jasmine said. "Let's just tell them the truth, tell them what happened. I mean, we didn't *make* Keysha get into the car and chase Anthony and we dang sure didn't cause the accident. So we can't be charged, right?" Jasmine looked around the room when no one said anything. "Right?"

Alexis shrugged. "Your guess is as good as mine. But it looks like we're about to find out," she said as the door opened slowly.

Rachel walked in, along with Officer Patterson and another man in regular clothes. He had a notepad and looked like one of those detectives on TV.

Rachel glared at each of us, the disappointment evident

in her eyes. "I am so upset with you girls," she finally said. Her words were slow and powerful. "I can not believe I'm down at the police station for you all—again."

She sat down at the head of the table. Both officers sat at the other end.

"As a favor to me, Detective Davis here"—she pointed to the male officer—"is going to take notes, off the record, then evaluate your story. We are hoping that your involvement was minimal and in no way criminal. Because neither your parents nor an attorney is present nothing you say will be held against you. But what you do say will determine if a formal investigation is launched. We are hoping that you can clear all of this up, and that way, there never has to be a formal investigation. Now who wants to tell me what happened?

"I want you to start at the very beginning," Rachel said. "No, I take that back because I know the beginning. We talked about that and I thought we had resolved to let this issue die. But since you girls just basically lied to me, someone pick up the story from there."

Nobody said anything. Rachel cleared her throat, her anger building. "I'm going to ask you again and this time we are not going to sit here and play dumb. Somebody better answer me or I will get up and walk out of here and let them throw you in a cell till your parents get here."

I didn't know if she was trying to scare us or what, but as far as I was concerned, it worked.

Camille sighed and with a defeated look across her face began the story from beginning to end. By the time she finished, Rachel looked even more disappointed. I didn't blame her. I was disappointed in myself just hearing it all over again.

"Girls, I guess I don't need to tell you how upset I am right now," Rachel said.

"No, you don't," Alexis said, speaking for all of us. "We should've listened to you."

"Yes, you should have. I mean, how would you have lived with yourself if both Keysha and her cousin had, God forbid, died in that accident? It's my understanding that they could have."

We didn't respond. We *couldn't* respond. I don't know about everybody else, but I would've been a basket case.

"This is exactly what I'm talking about in terms of the consequences of our actions. This is what can happen when we try to take vengeance into our own hands," Rachel went on. "And when would this cycle have stopped? What if the cops weren't there and Shoshanna and her friends had actually hurt you girls? Would you then have turned around and tried to get them back?"

We definitely didn't want to listen to a lecture, but I knew right about now we probably needed to hear one.

Rachel shook her head in disgust once again and looked to the end of the table. "Detective Davis, based on what the girls have told you, what does this mean?"

The silence filled the room. I was sure everyone could hear my heart beating, that's how scared I was. All I could think of was Angelica. My baby girl would have to come visit me in prison. My mom, who was old enough as it was, would be faced with raising her. And for what? All because I wanted to take part in paying some girl back over a boy? And he wasn't even my man. Dang, I had never thought about all the things that could happen from one little dumb idea.

But I couldn't even be mad at Alexis or Camille because I had just as eagerly jumped on board. I should've at least been a voice of reason. I was usually the rational one of the group.

"Well, I have to say this is an unusual case for me, Mrs. Adams," Detective Davis said. "Granted, they did not make those girls get in the car and speed down the highway, but they did incite the argument, much like one incites a riot. But based on what they told me, I don't think I have grounds to arrest or charge them. So I'm sure they'll be happy to know that they've gotten off with nothing more than a stern warning." He looked each of us dead in the eye before continuing. "Girls, be careful of playing dangerous games. Next time you might not be so lucky."

I tell you, if I knew how to do a backflip, I would have, right there in the middle of the conference room. I was so happy, the next thing I knew, I busted out crying. I couldn't help it.

"Let this be a valuable lesson to you girls," Officer Patterson added.

"Oh, believe me, it is," Camille said.

"You don't even know," Alexis added.

Jasmine didn't say a word. She just sat like she'd dodged a bullet and was still in shock.

"You need to get down on your knees and thank God for giving you ladies yet another chance," Rachel said as she stood. She walked to the end of the table and shook Detective Davis's hand. "Thank you very much for your time." She then leaned in and hugged her friend. "And of course, Lydia, as always, thank you for looking out for my girls."

"Hopefully, the fact that they're not getting arrested this time around will serve as inspiration enough for them to stay out of trouble," Officer Patterson sternly said.

"Oh, they're not out of trouble. They haven't even met trouble," Rachel said, eyeing all of us. "I have some plans for them that they're not going to be too thrilled about. And oh yeah, just so you know, I will be paying a visit to each of your parents."

"Miss Rachel, please," Jasmine begged. "Please don't say anything to my mom."

"Now, you know better than that," Rachel replied. "I've already called and left a message with your brother that I need to speak with your mother as soon as possible."

Jasmine groaned and a look crossed her face that said "Maybe jail wouldn't be so bad after all."

"You may have escaped the police but you'll have to endure whatever your parents and I have in store. And don't even bother begging because I'm not trying to hear it. You just better thank your lucky stars that you're walking out of here with me today instead of being escorted back to a cell."

We definitely couldn't argue with that. No matter what kind of trouble I got into back home, it was better than being locked up. I bit down on my lip as we followed her out.

24

Jasmine

We all stood outside Room 221 at Ben Taub Hospital. None of us wanted to go in, but at the same time, we knew that we needed to.

Rachel stood near the elevator. She was going down to the cafeteria to get a cup of coffee. Even if we did have the urge to bolt and never come back here, which I definitely wanted to do, Rachel wasn't having it. I turned toward her, pleading with my eyes for her not to make us go in there and face Keysha. Rachel shot me a look that told me we didn't have a choice before she disappeared into the elevator.

Rachel said even though we'd escaped any serious trouble from the police, we were still in big trouble with her.

Besides upping our community service, she made us come here to apologize in person to Keysha, who had been moved from Intensive Care and was now in a private room.

"Well, open the door," I whispered to Camille. "We might as well go on in. The sooner we got this over with, the better."

"Excuse me, may I help you?"

We turned toward the soft, yet tired voice. It was coming from an older woman; her hair was frazzled and all over her head. Her eyes had bags under them. She looked worn-out. "I'm Keysha's mother, Evelyn Miles. May I help you?"

We all kind of looked at one another. I finally nudged Camille, hoping she'd step up and say something. "Ummm, we . . . we just wanted to go in and check on Keysha."

Mrs. Miles sighed as she dabbed at her eyes. "Are you friends of hers?"

"Something like that," Camille said. "We just, ummm, we just wanted to see how she was doing."

"Oh, the Lord is keeping her hanging on," Mrs. Miles said wearily. "But it's been hard. We had to admit her father to the hospital yesterday. The stress of seeing his baby girl like this just took its toll. He already had a weak heart and for him to come so close to losing his baby, it just got to be too much."

Not only had we caused Keysha to be in this terrible accident, but we were inadvertently behind her father having a heart attack. Shoot, forget getting Keysha to forgive us. I wondered if God would forgive us.

"You know, it's so nice of you girls to come by and pay Keysha a visit," her mother continued. "She hasn't had many guests and I know that it would lift her spirits to know that her friends really care about her."

"Is she gonna be all right?" Alexis finally spoke up.

"We don't know," Keysha's mother answered. "The doctor said the accident severely damaged her spine. That means she may never walk again. What I just don't understand is why Keysha was flying around that freeway like that. She isn't a reckless driver. Never had a ticket in her life so I don't understand it."

We were all silent.

"But I guess it's not for me to understand. All I can do is give thanks. It could've been so much worse. God could've taken my baby. Her life may never be the same, but at least she'll be here with us." Mrs. Miles took a deep breath. "Well, look here, girls, I didn't mean to ramble on like this. Between my baby and my husband, I've just been so stressed out, but I guess God never gives us more than we can handle. You go on in and visit with Keysha. She just had her medication so she may be a little groggy, but you go on in. Thank you again."

Keysha's mother reached over and hugged each one of us. Angel was actually crying and I could see Camille and Alexis's eyes watering up as well.

"God bless you, babies. Enjoy your visit," she said before she left.

Now I definitely didn't want to go in there.

"Come on, you guys. Let's just get this over with," Angel said, leading the way.

We walked in. The sight of Keysha lying in the bed, her lower body in a cast, was heartbreaking. One of her arms was also wrapped in bandages and held up in the air by some steel-looking thing. There were tubes everywhere. We all watched her for a few minutes. Her eyes were closed and her chest was slowly heaving up and down.

Camille cleared her throat. "Keysha?" she whispered.

"Okay, she's sleep, y'all. Let's go," I quickly said. We were just about to leave when Keysha opened her eyes.

"What do you want?" she said, her voice sounding all scratchy.

"Ummm, w-we, ummm, we just wanted, these are my friends," Camille stammered.

"What? You came to gloat?" Keysha winced, as if a sudden burst of pain had shot through her body. "You came to see how you got me back?"

She pushed a button and took a deep breath. "I hope you're happy. You got what you wanted. Now get out of my room."

Camille stepped toward her. "Naw, Keysha, it's not like that at all."

Alexis walked up to her as well. "We just want to say we're sorry about everything."

Keysha looked Alexis up and down. "So you're the prissy one?" She let out a pained laugh. "You're sorry? About which part? Trying to steal my man? Setting all of this up? 'Cause I know y'all were behind it. Anthony said he never sent me a note." She looked away as her voice softened to a whisper and a small tear trickled down her cheek. "You got what you wanted. Payback. I'm never gonna walk again."

Alexis walked right up to her bed. "No, that's not what we wanted."

Keysha took a deep breath like she was trying to harden up. "I may be from the hood," she said, fighting back tears. "But I ain't stupid. You wanted me to go off on Anthony. You probably wanted both of us dead."

"Look, Keysha," Camille said, her voice full of sincerity, "we never meant for any of this to happen."

"I bet you didn't." She looked away. "But you got your payback. I'm sure that's all that matters to you. Now get out."

We all stood for a minute, feeling like there was something more we should say.

"We're really sorry," Alexis repeated.

"Yeah, you said that already. Now, get out," Keysha said with even more force. She didn't have to tell me again. This whole scene was making me sick to my stomach. I bolted toward the door. Camille, Alexis, and Angel quickly followed.

We'd hardly gotten outside of the hospital room, when we saw Anthony walking toward us, a big teddy bear and some balloons in his hands. He looked his usual handsome self, only his eyes were different. They looked tired and sad.

He stopped in his tracks when he saw us. "What are you all doing here?"

Alexis was the first to speak. "We . . . we just wanted to see how Keysha was doing."

Anthony shifted his weight, diverting his eyes to the floor. "I guess you saw, huh?"

An uncomfortable silence hung in the air. Finally, Camille said, "Look, Vic, I mean Anthony, we didn't mean for all of this to happen."

Anthony shrugged. "Whatever."

"Seriously," Alexis chimed in.

"Alexis, get out my face. You and your girl wanna talk about me, but you're no better than me. You tried to play me just like I played you." He looked back and forth between her and Camille. "So, I guess we're even. Too bad my girl is the one paying the price." He took a deep breath, and it looked like he was actually trying not to cry. "Look, I wasn't tryin' to hurt nobody.

"And just so you know, I wasn't messin' with Keysha when I was with you two. Not that it matters, but me and Keysha go way back. We've been together since the sixth grade. We escaped the hurricane together and when we moved to Houston, we made sure we ended up at the same school. But we kinda go back and forth, and when I met both of you, we weren't together."

I don't know why Anthony felt the need to come clean, but I could tell his words were getting to both Camille and Alexis.

"I just want this to be over. We didn't escape the hurricane to come to Houston and get killed over no stupidity," he continued. "And I made sure Shoshanna knew this beef is squashed, so y'all ain't gotta worry about nobody trying to get you back. Just let it go. For Keysha's sake."

Camille was about to say something when Keysha's mom came walking back up. "Anthony, baby. How are you today?" She hugged him and then looked at us. "Anthony is such a good boy. He's been here every day for Keysha. I think he's why she's fighting so hard to pull through this."

Anthony just stared at us, before turning to Mrs. Miles. "Come on, let's go check on Keysha," he said. "I brought her this." He held up the teddy bear and balloons.

They walked off without saying good-bye and we were left standing in the middle of the hospital hallway, feeling worse than we had before.

25

Jasmine

"So you guys were really the reason behind the accident? I mean, you set everything up?" Tameka's eyes were wide as saucers, like we'd really done something major. She'd asked us one hundred and one questions until we finally broke down and told her what had happened and what we were in trouble for.

"Dang! I gotta give it to you. That's tight. Why y'all always leavin' me outta stuff? I miss all the fun!"

I shook my head at her. "Tameka, there ain't been nothing fun about these last few days."

Besides the visit to the hospital, Rachel had made us miss our school's playoff football game on Saturday to go volunteer in the disabled children's unit at Texas Children's

Hospital. Man, that was depressing. Next week, we have to clean up a couple of parks in Fifth Ward, one of the older neighborhoods across town. Shoot, I did enough cleaning at home. I wasn't tryin' to spend my weekends cleaning.

"I know one thing. Miss Rachel is right," Alexis said, leaning back against the sofa in the den at her house. It was our monthly Good Girlz social night and honestly, we all could've passed on it, we were just that drained, but Rachel had been adamant that we still have the social night.

"Right about what?" Angel asked as she tucked her feet underneath her and tried to get comfortable on the floor.

"Right about leaving revenge to God. My payback days are over. It's just not worth it." Alexis sighed.

"Oh, here you go, getting all sanctified." Tameka rolled her eyes.

I debated saying something, but Tameka didn't know how rough these last few weeks had been, so she couldn't possibly understand. I definitely knew where Alexis was coming from.

I'd spent the whole past week listening to my mama and my grandma go off. When one of them stopped, the other would start up. My mother screamed, like she does most of the time. My grandmother lectured and quoted Bible scriptures around the clock. Over and over and over. And of course, my mom had to constantly remind me how she and my grandmother were working so hard to give me a better life and how I didn't appreciate anything and was willing to throw it all away just to get back at somebody.

My mother had put me on three months' punishment.

At least I'm too old to get spankings anymore. Although a few times, I sure thought she was gon' haul off and knock me out.

Both Angel and Camille's moms had pretty much spent the week lecturing them as well. Camille's mother had taken away her TV. The "no TV" rule meant she would miss the season finale of *America's Next Top Model*, and for Camille that was the same thing as beating her and throwing her in an abandoned cell.

Even Alexis, whose parents were usually the most lenient, had punished her by taking away her BMW. They made Alexis catch the bus wherever she needed to go.

It was actually funny when she arrived at last Thursday's meeting. First of all, she was an hour late. Then she walked in looking like she'd been in a hurricane. Her heel was broken (why she wore heels on a bus is beyond me) and her hair was all over her head (she said she'd had to run after the bus).

"I can not do public transportation," she'd moaned when she walked into the meeting. "Some man sat next to me who smelled like he hadn't had a bath in like, forever."

I actually laughed. I wished taking the bus was my biggest concern.

"So, what do you guys think about Keysha's news?" Angel asked, bringing me back to the now.

I couldn't help but feel another wave of relief rush through my body. Rachel had told us this morning that she'd found out that Keysha's new test results showed her injuries might not be as bad as her doctors initially thought. And although she still had a long road to recovery, she most likely would be able to walk again one day.

"I, for one, am so glad because I just would've felt awful if Keysha was paralyzed for life," Alexis said.

"I feel you there," I added, reflecting on how bad things could've been.

"Where's Camille?" Angel said, eyeing the tall grandfather clock in the corner of the den.

"Camille sent me a text earlier that said she was on her way. But you know her mom took her car, too, so she's catching the bus," Alexis told us, shivering at the thought.

We talked and joked around for a little while longer until the sound of an engine roaring into Alexis's circular driveway sent us all to the large window in the living room.

"Who's that?" Angel asked after we raised the blinds and peered outside.

Alexis shrugged. "I don't know anybody with a Trans Am, especially one that loud."

We watched as the fire red car came to a screeching halt and the passenger door opened. Camille bounced out, a huge grin across her face.

She waved good-bye to the driver, then came inside.

"Hey everybody, sorry I'm late," she said. "I had to wait forever on the bus."

"That didn't look like a bus to me," I said.

"It wasn't." She smiled wickedly. "That was Romeo."

"Who?" me and Angel said at the same time.

"I met him at the bus stop." She sighed dreamily. "He saw me waiting and offered me a ride."

"So now you're picking up strangers?" I asked, not even believing that after all the stuff we'd just gone through over Anthony, Camille still had boys on the brain.

"I didn't pick him up, he picked *me* up," she corrected, as she dropped her purse on the table in the foyer. "And he's not a stranger. His cousin lives down the street from me, so I've seen him around a lot. I just never really talked to him before now."

"How old is he?" Alexis asked.

"Nineteen." Camille pranced in and sat down on the sofa.

"Nineteen?" Angel laughed. "Yeah, right. Your mom is so not gonna let you date him."

"And he is sooooo cute," Camille continued, ignoring Angel. "I'm really feelin' him, and you know what?"

"Let me guess," I said, shaking my head. "You think you're in love."

"And you know this!" she exclaimed. "But this time, it's different . . . this time, it's for real."

She flashed a wide grin and I couldn't help but laugh. Some things would never change. And looking at my friends (and Tameka) gathered around chillin', I didn't think I'd ever want them to.

Reading Group Guide for

Getting Even

by ReShonda Tate Billingsley

Questions for Discussion

1. *Getting Even* is told from Jasmine's and Angel's point of view. Do you think this alternating point of view was an interesting way to tell a story focused on Camille and Alexis? Explain.

2. On page 9, when Shoshanna and Keysha confront Camille about dating Vic, Alexis hopes Camille will just walk away and not get into a fight. How would you have handled things?

3. When Jasmine realizes that Anthony and Vic are the same person, she does not immediately tell Alexis and Camille. Do you agree with her decision? Explain.

4. At what point did you begin to realize that Anthony and Vic were the same person? Is there anything you thought should have made the girls suspicious?

5. Does Vic/Anthony deserve payback? Ms. Rachel tells the girls that revenge is something we should leave up to God. Is there ever a time when revenge is okay?

6. Alexis is angry because she gave Anthony her chastity ring and was thinking of giving up her virginity to him. Why do you think she did not tell her friends or mention it to anyone else?

7. Friendship is a big part of this story. There are several times the girls wonder if their actions will cause problems or end their friendship. Do you think the girls have a strong bond?

8. The book begins and ends with Camille saying she thinks she is in love. Do you think she knows what being in love means? What does it mean to you?

9. Do you feel like the girls ultimately learned that they should think about their actions and how those actions can affect others?

Activities to Enhance Your Book Club

1. Before your book club meeting, take a stab at writing a short chapter on each character and where he or she will be in the future. Share your chapter with the group.

2. The Good Girlz decide to go out on their dates to Camille's favorite restaurant. For the next book club meeting, consider having everyone bring a favorite food.

3. Visit the author's MySpace page at http://www.myspace .com/goodgirlz1.

A Conversation with ReShonda Tate Billingsley

This is your fourth Good Girlz novel. How, if at all, was your writing process different from when you wrote the previous books?

I'm more into the characters now. Previously, I felt like I was getting to know them. But now I know them like the back of my hand. As for the writing itself, I'm now a full-time writer, whereas when I wrote the previous novels I was working as a television news reporter. I love the flexibility of writing full-time, but honestly, it's a little harder. You have to have discipline (and you *have* to stop watching *American Idol, America's Next Top Model,* and *Making the Band*—but I'm still working on that part!).

How did the story develop? Did you have the whole story in your head when you began writing? Did you draw inspiration from any real-life events or acquaintances?

I can never map out my entire story before I begin writing because the minute I do that, Jasmine will decide she wants to do something else. My characters take on a life of their own, so I just let the words take me where they decide to go. I'm always drawing from real-life experiences and events, and yes, I do have some of my friends' qualities in the book (although you'll never get me to admit that in a court of law!).

Are any of the secondary characters—Anthony, Keysha, Shoshanna—based on people you have come into contact with? Will you revisit these characters in future stories?

Anything's possible. It's funny, when I first started writing, Shoshanna was nowhere in the book, then all of a sudden, she just made an appearance, tapping me on my shoulder, saying, "Hey, lady, put me in the book!" I don't know anyone like her, while I do know people like Keysha, and definitely like Anthony!

Why is the novel written from Jasmine's and Angel's points of view when it's Camille's and Alexis's relationship with Anthony/Vic that is the focus of the story?

Because sometimes we're too close to a situation to see it through fully. We ignore signs we should be paying attention to because we're close. I wanted the readers to experience the story through Jasmine's and Angel's eyes so they could see how sometimes your friends can see things that you can't.

What lesson or feelings would you like readers to come away with?

Definitely forgiveness. A lot of times we get so wrapped up in "he [or she] did me wrong so now I have to get them back." I wanted to show how a quest for revenge doesn't do anything but lead to more problems. It's best to try to forgive a person (even if we don't forget). Too much negative energy goes into contemplating revenge.

Where and when do you write? How long does it take to write a book? Did you always want to be a writer?

I write in my office, at Starbucks, at the railroad tracks, in a boring meeting, while my infant son is sticking a cracker in my ear, you name it. I don't believe in idle time. I think that's how I'm able to churn out a book in one to three months. I have always loved writing. Even in elementary school, I used to get in trouble because I would make up stories. My teacher would say, "ReShonda, where's your homework?" Then I would proceed to tell her how I was walking to school, then saw a man with one leg mugging an old lady, so I had to take my notebook and beat him over the head with it and he used his one good leg to kick my notebook into the sewer and . . . Needless to say, my teachers didn't like that. I didn't consider myself untruthful; I just thought I was letting my imagination go to work!

In promoting the Good Girlz series, you have had the opportunity to meet and inspire many teens. Do you have any advice for young aspiring authors?

Don't talk about it, be about it. So many young people talk about what they want to do, whether it's writing a book or starting a business. But excuses always get in the way. "I'm too young," "I don't have the money," "No one believes in me." No matter what your dream is, stop talking about doing it and just do it. Find a way to make your dream a reality.

Will you write books for the young adult audience outside of the Good Girlz series?

I'm sure. I love writing for young adults, and at some point the Good Girlz will have to grow up. But I plan to continue writing positive, page-turning stories for young adults!

Will there be more stories based on the Good Girlz? And if so, what's next?

Absolutely! Camille, Alexis, Jasmine, and Angel are just juniors in high school. Senior year is coming up, so you know they'll be bringing the drama. Up next, the girls try out for a high school sorority, and when two of them make it and the other two don't—let's just say their friendship will truly be tested, especially when the real reason why one of them didn't make it is revealed. That's *Fair-Weather Friends* . . . check it out this fall!

Don't miss the next Good Girlz adventure

Fair-Weather Friends

Coming September 2008

Turn the page for a preview of
Fair-Weather Friends . . .

1

Camille

These chicks were off the chain!

I couldn't do anything but stare in awe at the twelve girls on the auditorium stage. Not only did they look cute as all get-out in their tight black low-riders and pink T-shirts with "Theta Diva" spelled out in rhinestones, but they were doing moves I'd never seen before.

As a member of my high school's drill team, I can appreciate a good dancer, but these girls were dancing and stepping like they were starring in that *Stomp the Yard* movie. They had the crowd going wild.

One of my best friends, Alexis, must've been thinking the same thing because she leaned in to me and shouted over the thumping rap music, "Girl, what's the name of this group again?"

"They're called the Theta Ladies. It's a sorority at my school," I responded as we stood with the crowd and applauded like crazy while the girls exited the stage.

Although they were on campus at a lot of other schools here in Houston, the Thetas had just started at my school last year. I'd seen the girls around campus, wearing their pink-and-white T-shirts, but I'd never paid them much attention. Until now.

"Gimme a break. They ain't all that," my other best friend Jasmine said as she turned up her nose. I ignored her. Jasmine always had something negative to say. Not many things impressed her and she always found something wrong with everything.

Jasmine had come a long way from when we first met her a year and a half ago, though. That's when we all joined the Good Girlz, a community service group formed by Rachel Jackson Adams, the first lady of this church in our neighborhood.

I know the name may sound a little hokey, but don't get it twisted. We aren't some goody-two-shoes group. In fact, Miss Rachel started the group as part of some youth outreach program at Zion Hill Missionary Baptist Church, where her husband was pastor. Even though her daddy was a preacher, Miss Rachel was buck-wild as a teenager; now that she was grown, she wanted to do something to help teens who were headed down the wrong path. And boy, were we headed down the wrong path.

I was actually facing jail time when I hooked up with the Good Girlz. It's almost unbelievable since I had never been in any major trouble before that, but the dog who used to be my boyfriend had my nose wide open. Six months after me and Keith started going together, he got arrested for carjacking an old lady. He kept saying he didn't do it. I believed him, but he couldn't wait for justice to prevail so he broke out of jail. (We later found out he really didn't do it. It was his stepbrother.) After he escaped, Keith had me hide him at my grandma's house. The thing was, I didn't even know he'd broken out. He told me they let him go. Anyway, the police eventually found him at my grandma's and that fool took off through a back window and left me to take the rap for hiding him.

So when the judge told me it was either jail or the Good Girlz—well, you can see that was a no-brainer. Let me just tell you, I'm too cute for jail. (People tell me all the time I look like a prettier version of Kyla Pratt, that girl who played on the TV show *One on One*.)

It's a good thing I joined the Good Girlz because the police later found Keith hiding out at his baby mama's house. Did I mention that I didn't know he had a baby? Or a baby mama? So, I probably would've been in prison for real for killing him if it wasn't for the Good Girlz.

"Look how they're strutting around like they're all that." Jasmine's voice snapped me out of my thoughts.

I grinned as I watched the Thetas walk down the aisle. Everyone was stopping them and giving them props. "They are all that," I said, my voice full of admiration.

"Really, they're not," Jasmine snarled.

I blew her off because Jasmine was my girl, funky attitude and all. Miss Rachel had made Jasmine join the Good Girlz after breaking up a fight between her and this boy named Dedrick. At six feet tall and two hundred plus pounds, Jasmine wasn't anybody you wanted to mess with. Just ask Dedrick. She had beat him like he stole something just because he was teasing her.

Jasmine had actually toned down some of her mean ways over the last year and a half. Although you'd never know it by the way she was sitting over there with her nose all turned up.

"I didn't know they even had sororities in high school," Alexis said.

Alexis was the rich girl of the group. Her dad is some big-time businessman and her family has beaucoup money. She resembled Beyoncé (and didn't hesitate to let you know it) and was always dressed in the tightest clothes, looking like she had just stepped off the cover of a magazine. But she's so cool that her bourgie ways don't bother me. Most of the time anyway.

I turned my attention back to Alexis, since she was just as hyped as I was.

"Yeah, lots of high schools have sororities," I said.

"Have you ever thought about joining?" the fourth member of our group, Angel, leaned in and asked. She'd been so quiet I'd almost forgotten she was there. But that was Angel's nature. She was the sweet, quiet one of the group. Getting pregnant at fifteen had made her grow up pretty fast, especially because her baby's daddy was this tri-flin' boy named Marcus, who didn't even claim his and Angel's daughter Angelica. I loved Angel and her daughter was so adorable, but I wouldn't trade places with her for anything in the world.

"I think it would be cool to be a Theta," Alexis wistfully said. "But they don't have them at my school."

Alexis was the only one of us who didn't go to Madison High School. She went to a private school called St. Pius on the other side of town.

"I told you about that new rule the school district has that lets students participate in extracurricular activities at another school if your school doesn't offer it," I said. "So, you could join the Thetas at our school."

"For real?" she asked, wide-eyed.

I nodded as the next sorority made their way onto the stage. Sure, I'd watch them perform but for me, the Thetas had already stolen the show.

2

Camille

I couldn't stop talking about the Theta Ladies. As a matter of fact, the whole school was talking about them. Surprisingly, they didn't win first place in the step show. They'd come in second behind a sorority from Booker T. Washington High School. Even so, the boys had been all over them like they were celebrities or something.

I'd filled in our fellow Good Girlz member, Tameka (she was Miss Rachel's niece and had joined the group about six months after we started), about the show and now she was just as hyped as me, and sick that she'd missed it in the first place.

"Dang, I didn't know the Thetas had it goin' on like that," she said. "I can't believe I missed it."

"You ought to quit sneaking out of the house. Then maybe you wouldn't be on punishment all the time." I laughed.

"Now, see, you asking too much," she joked.

Even though me, Jasmine, Alexis, and Angel weren't as close to Tameka as we were to one another, she was still cool and I was glad to see she was worked up about the Thetas, too.

Jasmine had gotten tired of hearing me rave about them, but Angel and Alexis were still excited. Me and Angel were rehashing to Tameka our favorite parts of the show as we made our way into the pizza line in the school cafeteria.

"Hey, isn't that the girl who was leading the Theta's step team this weekend?" Angel whispered as we grabbed our trays. I looked up to see who she was talking about: a tall, pretty, mocha-skinned girl who was at the front of the line.

"Yeah. Her name is Raquelle. She's on the drill team with me," I replied.

"Isn't that Tori Young next to her? She wasn't in the show, was she?" Angel asked.

"I didn't see her, but maybe she was in the back or something," I answered.

I was glad that Jasmine wasn't here. She usually ate lunch with us but she had to take a makeup test today. Jasmine and Tori didn't get along. Then again, there weren't too many people who Jasmine did get along with. But Tori and Jasmine were definitely like oil and water. Mainly because of Donovan, Jasmine's ex-boyfriend. He was in college now, but when he transferred here last year from New Orleans after Hurricane Katrina, Tori had set her sights on him. Only, he was trying to get with Jasmine and wouldn't give Tori the time of day. She definitely couldn't appreciate that. She and Jasmine had almost come to blows several times behind him.

"I knew she was a Theta," I told Angel as we paid for our pizza. "But I just found out yesterday that she's actually the president."

"Wow. They look so cute in those jackets," Tameka said, admiring the thin pink satin jackets with the word "Theta" on the front and a white poodle, which was their mascot, on the back. It was hot outside, but inside, our buildings were always freezing, so they didn't look out of place in their jackets.

"Are you guys going over there?" Tameka said.

I debated for a minute. "Maybe I'll just say hi as we pass by."

Tameka looked at her watch. "Dang, I have got to get to detention. I wanted to go talk to them."

"Girl, you'd better go," I said. "You know Mr. Matthews said he was going to add two more weeks of detention if you were late again."

Tameka huffed like life was so unfair as she told us bye and headed out of the lunch room.

We made our way toward our normal seats in the back of the cafeteria. I caught eyes with Raquelle as we passed the Theta table. I didn't want to be jockin' anybody, but I did want to let them know how tight their show had been.

"Hey, Raquelle," I said, stopping in front of their table. She was sitting with Tori and several other girls. All of them were wearing the Theta jackets. "I just wanted to tell you all that show you did this weekend was off the hook."

Raquelle smiled. "Thanks."

"And you all were definitely robbed," I continued. "Everybody knows you guys should've won first place."

She looked at the other girls and giggled. "Tell me about it."

"Isn't your name Camille?" one of the girls sitting on the side of Raquelle asked me.

"Yeah, Camille Harris. And this is my friend Angel Lopez," I said, pointing to Angel, who waved meekly.

"You're on the drill team, aren't you?" another girl asked, all but ignoring Angel.

I nodded.

"Well, I'm Lynn. I'm vice president of the Thetas." She pointed to the other four girls. "And this is Constance, Claudia, Alisha, and Tori."

"Oh, I know Camille very well," Tori snidely remarked.

I'd been around a couple of the times Tori had gotten into it with Jasmine so she definitely knew who I was. I smiled anyway. I didn't have a beef with Tori and I wasn't about to start now.

"Do you wanna sit with us?" Raquelle asked.

My mouth almost hit the floor. I knew the sorority girls could get a little snooty and they really didn't like anyone invading their clique. So I was thrilled that they wanted us to sit with them.

"Sure, we'd love to sit with you guys," I said.

Me and Angel sat down in two empty seats across from Raquelle. I couldn't be sure, but it looked like Tori and Claudia shot Angel a crazy look as she sat down. It made me uncomfortable for a minute, but then I told myself I was just imagining things.

"So how long have you guys been Thetas?" I asked as I bit into my pizza.

"We all joined last year when we started the organization here at Madison," Lynn said.

"Do you all practice a lot to be able to step like that?" I asked.

Lynn smiled. "We do. But there is so much more to us than stepping. We actually do a lot of community service. You should check out our MySpace page and see what we're all about."

"I'll definitely do that."

I wrote down their MySpace address on the back of my geometry folder.

We talked and laughed the rest of the lunch period. I know a lot of people thought the Thetas were snobs, but I really liked them. We seemed to click.

I was kinda bummed when the bell rang, signaling the end of lunch. We had been hitting it off so well I hated to see it end.

"Well, I gotta go. I got a test in Chemistry next period," Lynn said as she stood up. "Camille, it was nice meeting you. I've seen you around school but I didn't know you were so cool."

I smiled and waved good-bye to her and the other girls. Even Tori had warmed up to me and smiled as she walked off.

I turned to Angel. "That was so cool," I said.

"For you, maybe," Angel replied, standing up and grabbing her tray.

I stood up, too. "What do you mean?"

Angel turned toward me. She had a disgusted look on her face. "Am I invisible? Nobody said two words to me the entire time."

I tried to laugh it off. Now that I thought about it, no one had really talked to Angel, but it was probably just because she was so quiet herself.

"You weren't talking either," I said, playfully pushing her shoulder. Even though Angel was cute with her long, jet-black hair, olive-colored skin, and light brown eyes, she definitely lacked in the confidence department. The Thetas probably just picked up on that. "You know you're all shy and stuff. They talk so much, they probably didn't even pay you any attention."

"Exactly," she snidely replied.

"I didn't mean it like that. You know it takes you a minute to warm up to people."

She shrugged as she walked over and tossed her plate in the trash. "I guess. I mean, they are cool and all, but I'm not getting a good vibe from them."

I followed her and threw my trash away as well. "Come on, you're starting to sound like Jasmine. I think you're overreacting. They just need to get to know the Angel we all know and love."

She finally smiled. "I guess you're right."

I wrapped my arm through hers as we made our way through the crowd of students filing out of the cafeteria. "I know I am. And now, more than ever, I'm sure about it."

"Sure about what?"

I dropped her arm, looked at her, and grinned. "We need to be Thetas."

She screwed up her lips. "Yeah, right."

"I'm serious."

Angel looked like she was thinking about it. "That would be tight, wouldn't it?"

"It would be especially tight if me, you, Jasmine, Alexis, and even Tameka were all Thetas."

Angel nodded. "It would be great to be in a sorority." The smile suddenly left her face and she looked at me skeptically. "Alexis, I can see. Even Tameka. But good luck getting Jasmine to go for the idea."

I smiled slyly. "You just leave that to me. I'll get Jasmine to come around."

Angel shrugged like she'd believe it when she saw it. Despite my outward confidence, I knew getting Jasmine to warm to the idea of joining the Thetas would be easier said than done.